I0606516

Acknowledgements

First and foremost, I must acknowledge my wife, Patty. You have been a great writing partner, story collaborator, editor, and muse. I appreciate that you see the world so differently than I. That difference keeps me on my toes. You have made the entire writing and living processes fun.

I also must acknowledge Aurelia Sands Wilson, my editor, my mentor, and my good friend of many years. I have learned so much from you. It has been an adventure. I couldn't have done it without you. You're the best.

The Defect

By Jeff Bailey

Chapter One

The oldie, *Help Me Rhonda*, by the Beach Boys blared from the cab of the pickup truck as it pulled into a spot in the employee parking lot of the Desert Canyons Nuclear Power Station in Southern California. Brian Sing rolled up the driver's side window with enough slow deliberation to let the song have time to finish. He liked surfing music. It was happy innocent, and the infectious beat always lightened his mood. When the DJ started talking, Brian shut off the engine and stepped out of the truck. Out of habit, he turned to face the open truck door and took a deep breath. The air was cool. He liked the springtime scent of the barrel cactus flowers carried by the late-night desert air. It was 11:45 p.m., and he had already passed through the security gate at the front of the facility. This was, for Brian, a conscious moment of transition. This was the moment he put the rest of the world out of his mind, put on his hard hat, and started his workday. Brian loved this moment because it was the start of his workday as an Operations Shift Supervisor at a nuclear power plant: one of the most technically demanding and interesting professions on Earth.

*****

At the same moment, a temporary employee named Alex James approached the Maintenance Building's riverside, emergency exit from the inside. He took out the stolen security badge that would allow him to open the exit without setting off the alarms. Alex's biggest concern, at the moment, was if he could find the .45 automatic handgun in the dark. If he could find it in the dark, he was certain he could find it in the middle of the morning, a few days from now.

*****

As Brian turned to face the nuclear facility, he began scanning the indicators of the operating conditions at the plant, taking in information. None of the cars in the parking lot to his left belonged to upper management. Nothing was going on in the power plant that required upper management supervision. Nice. To his right, the twin four hundred and ninety-nine-foot water cooling towers hummed, rumbled, and gurgled with a satisfying rhythm. The towers transferred waste heat from the power plant into the water in the towers and, ultimately, into the air above the plant. The waste heat dissipated into the passing breeze as opposed to dissipating into the nearby river. Brian could tell by the amount of steam, coupled with the current temperature and dew point, that the power station's main generator was operating at close to full power. These were both good omens for a nice, quiet shift. In a week, on May 1st, operators would shut down Desert Canyons for a refueling outage. For weeks thereafter, there would be no 'quiet' shifts.

As Brian approached the side door of the Turbine Building near the main transformer yard, he heard and felt the sound and vibration coming from the main turbine-generator. It was strong, invasive, persistent, and satisfyingly steady. He searched the TG's vibration for a low pulsing harmonic. If the vibrations had a low harmonic component (a slow, rhythmic pulsing), it might indicate that one of the bearings or blades of the turbine generator might be starting to wear. An unbalanced bearing or blade was not a good thing. Again, no detectible harmonic was a good omen for a quiet eight-hour shift.

Brian also felt for the lesser rumble of an operating emergency diesel generator. He could feel that there was no emergency diesel generator operating. The realization brought an even bigger smile to his face.

As Brian walked on, he continued to absorb data about the plant. The main transformer yard was deserted. The illuminated lights atop the main transformers indicated that they were online. All the main electrical distribution busses were energized. Brian saw no steam plume coming from the vent twenty feet above the ground at the back corner of the building. The steam-powered still that provided the facility's demineralized water, was not in operations. There was plenty of the ultra-pure, fresh water.

As he walked, Brian's data collection and evaluation routine never stopped. He turned off the parking lot and onto the sidewalk that led to the Turbine Building's riverside emergency exit. This single-wide, metal personnel door satisfied the legal requirement for an emergency fire exit. This face of the Turbine Building extended one hundred and thirty feet to the right and one hundred and seventy feet to the left. It was near eight stories tall, had no windows, and only one door. The plant designers wouldn't have included this door if the fire codes had not required it. The remaining visible features were a couple of piping vents, and the sets of security lights and cameras mounted fifteen feet off the ground on the corners of the building. This outside face of the Turbine Building was a vertical cliff of dark blue steel siding. The smallest face of the two-story Maintenance Building was visible beyond the left corner of the Turbine Building. A single exit door was the single architectural feature on the face of the Maintenance Building, as well. Except in the case of a fire, most personnel entered and exited the Desert Canyons facility through the Personnel Access Center at the front of the complex.

Out of routine, when Brian reached the turbine-building exit, he stopped and looked back at the parking lot and to the desert beyond. Everything was normal. He noticed Damaskenos Alexandrukus Xenakis (known to everyone as Dax) getting out of his car. Dax had a huge name, a huge personality to match, and was immensely popular at the Desert Canyons Facilities. The young ladies at Desert Canyons had nicknamed him 'Dax, something Greek.' Dax was a floor-operator-in-training on Brian's shift, and showed more natural talent as an operator than the two qualified floor operators who were training him.

Most shifts had trainees. Management expected operators at all levels to train their replacements. When a trainee passed his boards at any level, his trainer was qualified to become a trainee at the next higher level. It was management's practice to assign a trainee to the newly-qualified operator at the same time. The result was a never-ending supply of new operators. Training never stopped.

During Brian's shift, he was responsible for everything that occurred in the plant. For the next eight hours, the 'operations buck' stopped with Brian Sing. On Brian's shift, there was a control room operator who performed all the plant operating functions in the control room. Two floor operators rounded out the shift. They performed all the plant operating functions outside the control room. They were Brian Sing's auxiliary eyes, ears, and hands outside the control room during the shift. Dax was the sole trainee on the shift.

As Brian turned back to the open door, a movement at the maintenance building exit caught his eye. Someone was coming out of the Maintenance Building emergency exit. They used a key card and had computer authority to open the door, because no alarm sounded when the door opened. While it wasn't against the rules, per se, it was unusual. There was no doorknob, security badge slider, or keypad on the outside of the maintenance building exit. Anybody could exit, because it was opened from the inside. Most of the maintenance staff had gotten stuck outside at least once and had learned to not use the door. Brian couldn't see who exited, but figured that it was one of the temporary maintenance staff working late. Because of the refueling outage next week, the maintenance staff and temporary hires were putting in a lot of overtime with planning and scheduling every detail. Every minute that the plant wasn't producing electricity was a minute of lost revenue. Scheduling for the shortest shut-down possible was a nightmare. Whoever just came out the emergency exit wasn't as out of place as he would have been if no temporary staff was being utilized.

Brian recalled a lunch that he had with Lenell Spector a week earlier. Lenell was the administrative assistant to Richard Swift, the chief of plant security at Desert Canyon. Lenell had noticed some anomalies in the security/access reporting system and talked to Brian about them.

The security system logged the date, time, and person's name for every door-open event in the plant. Over the preceding few weeks, the logging system had logged the wrong person through the right door several times. When Lenell mentioned the anomalies to Richard, he didn't seem to think there was a concern because the building perimeter security wasn't involved, and the person logged in was always a staff member. To Lenell, though, Richard Swift's lack of alarm was almost a violation of his job description. The next logical assumption was that if there was a programming error, what other mistakes might the program make in a more serious situation? Lenell was concerned on several levels and told Brian about her concerns. Seeing a person exit the Maintenance Building at midnight was a little unusual, but Brian was pleased to have an opportunity to interact with Lenell again… in a professional capacity, of course. He would mention his observation to her at the first opportunity.

Brian stepped inside the Turbine Building and let the door close behind him.

*****

At the Maintenance Building emergency exit, Alex James, alias Adawi Aimur-Noor Kuzbari, The Son of the Lion, took a quick, nervous glance back at Sing. Alex wasn't a member of the permanent plant staff, and he didn't have the authority to open the maintenance building exit, especially since he was using someone else's access badge. Alex sighed with relief as Sing continued into the Turbine Building, and the exit door closed behind him. *Praise be to Allah*, Alex's luck held. It took a long moment for Alex to calm his fluttering heart and clear his vision. After a few seconds, he continued walking, not to the parking lot, but to the River Water Pump House, a little more than two hundred yards away. He started his stopwatch and continued taking notes. It was ninety-five steps and about forty seconds to where the semiautomatic pistol in its vacuum-sealed plastic bag lay hidden in the rocks at the side of the road. No, Alex didn't belong here.

*****

Once inside the Turbine Building, Brian walked around the base of the Main Condenser. The condenser was an eighty-foot long and fifty-five-foot-wide box hanging on the bottom of the main turbine. It contained racks of cooling tubes. Once the main steam did its work in the main turbine, it discharged into the condenser, where it was flash-cooled and condensed back into water. Three huge Reactor Feed Pumps then pumped the condensed water back through the hot reactor to be made back into steam. As Brian walked, he listened for the telltale whistle of a vacuum leak and looked for a puddle of condensate where it shouldn't be. *I love my job* he thought to himself. *I do love my job.*

Brian walked up the northeast stairs and onto the main turbine generator deck. The walls and floor were a shiny, white epoxy paint that provided a rugged, sealed surface. Huge halogen ceiling lamps lit the space like an NFL football stadium on game night. The air was hot and smelled of seared, hot metal and steam. There was no smoke or fire, just the scent of hot steel, like the smell of an automobile engine that had run too long without cooling water. There was also a faint background odor of machine oil (from the turbine bearings) and ozone (from the massive electric generator). The main turbine generator deck was a huge (three hundred fifty feet long, one hundred sixty feet wide, and three stories tall), imposing space. The sheer volume of the main turbine deck overwhelmed many first-time visitors: the size of the equipment and the assault on the senses of the light, heat, oil, and ozone.

Brian, however, was right at home. He was comfortable here, one of a new breed of nuclear power plant operators. The old breed. or 'old guard,' grew up with nuclear power plants. Archaic thinking taught the old guard to memorize preapproved procedures and to perform those procedures without question or analytical thought. "This light goes on, push that button. Keep the water level in the steam generators at 108 inches at all times– at ALL times". The members of the old guard were competent nuclear power plant operators if every conceivable event was covered by an approved procedure. They knew when to do what according to the correct procedures, but they had little or no 'feel' for the living, breathing nuclear power plant. They had difficulty knowing how to react in situations not included in the approved procedures. Brian Sing was a new guard operator. He had a 'feel' for the power plant, or, as the popular cartoon described it, he had 'the knack.' He knew how a subtle change in one system could affect another system. Brian always followed procedure, of course, but he was also aware of the thousand and one little ripples that his actions created throughout the rest of the plant. Brian was the epitome of the 'new breed.'

One could tell the different operating styles between the old guard and the new by watching the people in a control room if the overhead lights blinked. A blink in the lights might mean a surge or correction in electricity production, or it could mean the auto start of a pump after the failure of another pump or a tripped main turbine. In the worst case, it could mean a reactor 'Scram,' the immediate and complete shutdown of the nuclear reactor. A little blink of the control lights, and the 'new guard' operators would be up and on high alert, looking for the trend in voltage, temperature, pressure, or reactivity that might be a clue to the cause of the blink. They would attempt to find the trend before something undesirable happened, and act accordingly. The 'old guard' might also be on their feet, but they would wait for the alarms to go off and the annunciators to tell them what was going on. Then, the old guard would follow the appropriate procedure. Brian flashed on this difference in operating style as he walked around the end of the main turbine and prepared to enter the main control room.

Just before he entered the control room, Brian looked back out onto the turbine deck. He thought about the hundreds of thousands of parts that went into a nuclear power plant, the miles of pipe and wire, computers, gauges, meters, valves, *et cetera ad infinitum*, all working together. One of the smallest and most innocent items of all was the electric solenoid operated valve. It was similar in operation to a home irrigation system valve: apply electricity, the electric coil energizes, and the valve changes position. What was once closed opened. What was once open closed. Air, water, oil, and nitrogen, or some other liquid or gas, flowed or stopped flowing accordingly.

*****

The solenoid-operated air control valves at Desert Canyons were manufactured at a small, family-owned company in Conyers, Georgia. One batch of solenoid valves was assembled on October 22nd, 2003, as part of a special order from a prime contractor in California. They had been assembled during the day shift, but it fell to the night shift to test the solenoid valves and complete the quality QA1 paperwork for each valve.

This batch of valves was not physically different from any other batch of like-kind valves. The differrence defined by the QA1 designation was in the level of documentation. Every step in the assembly and testing sequence was signed for and documented. The employee that screwed the cover cap on the solenoid housing signed his name and date on the document package. The employee who polished the burrs off the valve seat signed his name and date on the document package. The employee who inserted the guide ring spacer signed his name and date on the document package. QA1 also required extra testing. Each document package had a signature block and a pass/fail box. Some had already been spot checked after assembly, but he had to test every single valve in a QA1 batch. It was time-consuming, tedious, and mind-numbing work, which was why it was done on second shift. Bobby Joe was assigned to the task because it was boring, repetitive, and monotonous.

Bobby Joe was the low man in the shop on night shift. He was paid minimum wage, had a bad attitude, and was a raving junkie. He was, however, a functional junkie. He could be comatose and those around him wouldn't notice. That was the case on this night. He was stoned, almost catatonic. Nobody cared. Nobody wanted to be stuck testing the solenoid valves. Bobby Joe didn't care, either. The way he figured, minimum wage meant minimum effort. He also thought that enough of the valves had been tested after assembly to verify that they were all good. He felt that he was wasting his minimum wage time.

Bobby Joe's singular obsessive desire on Earth was to go on a smoke break and reinforce his fading buzz. He connected the test clips to the next valve and pushed the button to start the automated test. *Whoa*, he was starting to feel his hands again. He didn't like feeling his hands. As soon as the test started, he put his head back and closed his eyes. He loved the sensation of spinning a few feet off the floor. He loved the high. He didn't see the 'Fail' LED come on. He didn't react to the faint 'ping' of the testing unit signifying a failure. It didn't register in his conscious mind that the valve stuttered instead of snapped as it closed. He didn't know that a thin, brass guide ring spacer had been bent during assembly. He didn't care. He floated and spun in a warm, all-encompassing bliss.

He closed his eyes for so long that the test unit reset and went dormant. When he looked back at the work table from within the dissipating fog, the LED was dark. He tried to remember if he heard a ping, but maybe not. He shrugged it off and signed the paperwork. Odds were, the valve had passed at least one test and would be tested a dozen more times before it was installed. Minimum wage bought minimum effort. By coincidence, the purchaser of this batch of valves had discontinued site testing of solenoid valves that had been factory-tested to save money (maximize profit). Boy, Bobby Joe wished he could take a smoke break.

At the end of the evening, the valves were packaged and shipped to Reason and Snelling Inc., the prime construction contractor at the constru-ction site at Desert Canyons, Cali-fornia. The valve was one minor part lost in the thousands of parts.

*****

Brian turned to the door and entered the control room. The first order of business was to relieve the previous Operations Shift Supervisor and take responsibility for the power plant. How Brian relieved his prede-cessor depended on who his prede-cessor was and what 'breed' of ope-rator he was. Brian stepped into the control room.

"Good evening, Sing," Matt Downing called as he rushed over. "How're ya' doin'? Running a little late tonight, are we?" Downing knew that the schedule for the swing shift was 4:00 p.m. to midnight, and that the shift ended at midnight, not ten seconds after midnight.

"Fine, feeling good," Sing replied with a smile as he scanned the control room, "It's a beautiful night. Want to stick around and pull a double shift?" He knew what the answer would be before Downing did, *Nope, done my duty.*

Downing guffawed, "Nope. My eight hours are up." Close enough.

"Okay, I'm listening. What's the status (*let's look at the logbook*)?" Brian said, while staring at Downing. It was time for the turnover status report.

"Let's look at the logbook," Downing answered as he walked to the central operating desk and picked up the logbook.

The turnover status report was a concise, verbal listing of what equipment was operating normally, operating abnormally, broken down, red tagged for maintenance, and anything else unusual. The report also identified any unusual people or groups of people working in the facility. An outgoing Operations Shift Supervisor should be able to recite the turnover report from memory. Downing read the report from the logbook.

"The logbook says that emergency diesel generator number two is red tagged for maintenance (it's in the logbook)?" noted Sing. Red tags were put on equipment to notify everyone that it shouldn't be touched, much less operated, by anyone other than the person designated on the tag.

Brian asked, "When was the diesel tagged out?"

"It's in the logbook," Downing was in a hurry.

After a couple more minutes of this formality, Brian said, "Okay, I've got the plant," and turned to make the log entry that transferred 'the buck' to him. When he turned back around, Downing was gone. That was all right. Sing knew most of what he needed to know. He would scout around the rest of the plant during the night's quiet moments and make his small, grease-pencil marks on the gauges. He would wander the halls and peer into the corners. It should be a quiet shift, routine to the point of boring.

Brian finished his last midnight shift at 8:00 a.m. This was Brian's last shift in the midnight rotation. At 8:00 a.m., in seventy-two hours, he would start a seven-day rotation of day shifts, but, for now, he drove home and ate a breakfast of tuna steak and salad. *How dull*, he thought. He knew he was a home-body. He suspected that it was time for him, a well-established, thirty-five-year-old bachelor, to get married and to start the 'family' part of his life. He felt the instinctive lure of a larger garden, a family dog, two to four children, and a wife's pretty smile. Thoughts of a wife led to thoughts of Lenell Spector.

"Oh rats!" he said aloud.

He had forgotten to stop by Lenell's office before he left the plant. He thought back to last night's 'door-open' event. It might prove significant. He also wanted to see Lenell again.

For now, breakfast was over, and it was time to sleep.

*****

As Brian headed for bed, Lenell was sitting down in her cubbyhole of an office. With a staff of one hundred and eighty-six, everyone in management had a private office. Some were just larger than others. Lenell's windowless office was small, and had tacky indoor/outdoor carpet, but she was here to work, not bask in luxury. Several pictures of Lenell's early American ancestors adorned the walls. Looking at her pictures soothed Lenell. She liked how they made her feel connected. Her favorite was the class picture for the one-room schoolhouse circa 1890. It showed two of Lenell's great-grandparents as eight- and nine-year-old students. Ironically, those two didn't marry each other; they married someone else who wasn't in the picture. Lenell finished her morning routine and stopped to look at her great-grandmother for a long minute. She turned to her computer and requested a door access report from the security access database. The rash of unexplained door access entries was always in the back of her mind. She was certain that there was something to the anomalies. She systematically eliminated all the 'door-open' events for the operating and maintenance staffs who were scheduled to be on-site and were where they were supposed to be. The names that remained were either the wrong people or the right people in the wrong place. The first thing she noticed was that Brian Sing accessed doors all over the plant, but Brian's job description included roaming the plant during his shift, so these entries were valid. She smiled as she crossed out the references to his name in the report.

Brian was tall, thin, dark (maybe Middle Eastern), and nice in a socially awkward, nerd-engineering way. He had a remarkable memory for technical details from how he programmed his first home computer, to how nuclear isotopes decayed after a nuclear fission. On the socially awkward side, he had once forgotten her name when he tried to introduce her to a colleague after having known her for almost a month. Being a people person, Lenell found the 'nerdy' side of engineers a little irritating. With Brian, though, it was endearing and cute.

"Okay, okay. Focus on the readouts," she mumbled to herself. On average, there were no more than one or two bogus entries per night. On the most recent night shifts, if one questionable entry were on the report, there would be a string of questionable entries, and last night was one of those nights. There was a string of door access entries in four different buildings over a two-hour period. The names listed on the door access report were impossible. Two of them weren't at the plant last night. One was a secretary in the retirement investments office downtown who had no legitimate business at the plant. The access program shouldn't have authorized any doors to be opened for her. Lenell noticed a new trend in the new strings of bogus entries. If she put the access times in chronological order, they looked like one person moving about the plant using other people's badges. Lenell thought the one person theory was improbable, though. No one person could accumulate so many badges from so diverse a collection of people.

She was stumped and did not like it. The most obvious explanation, and the most reasonable, was that the security program had a logic defect. An equally improbable explanation was that someone was confusing the entries on purpose, but the program would log intentional changes to the data and there were none. She even tried to make a change one afternoon with the intention of deleting the change log. She was able to change an entry in the database, but it made a log entry of the change and then denied her attempt to delete her entry. Outside of her boss, Richard Swift, a mere six employees in the downtown office could delete or change a record

Could Richard be the culprit? That idea seemed ridiculous. The other nagging question was, "Why?" No damage was ever done. Nothing was ever taken or disturbed. As always, the simple solution seemed to be the correct solution, which meant the security system's program was defective. She was waiting for the day that her name showed up in the access report as a bogus entry. She put the report in her bottom desk drawer with the previous reports. She would address this issue later.

*****

While Lenell pondered the bogus door entry problem, Manuel Rojas sat at his computer in the downtown personnel office. Manuel was a man whose life had been quagmired by anger and resentment. He was overlooked at work, underappreciated by management, and ignored by most of his coworkers. Even his wife thought he was strange at times. He religiously kept his anger pushed deep down inside where it was dark, and he displayed a 'happy face.' In the last few weeks, though, Manuel had found an outlet for his pent-up bile. He was happy to monitor the computer-to-computer door access requests as they occurred in the home office 'Personnel Tracking' database. He changed the data in the database at predetermined times since midnight. Now, he waited with smug satisfaction for one last data action.

As soon as Manuel saw a daily access report request from Lenell Spector, he made a flurry of data corrections and then deleted all permanent record of the changes he made. Manuel Rojas was being paid a great deal of money to manipulate the database. When he retired rich, he would not be angry anymore.

A man named Josef had approached Manuel and explained to him that the door access security system at Desert Canyons was a 'lookup' program. When someone swiped a badge to request access, the security system recorded the personnel ID number from the badge. The security system also logged the door number, date, and time. Then, the security system electronically accessed the central personnel database at the utilities' downtown office on a dedicated phone line to see if the person with that ID number was authorized to access that door. The central security system looked up the level of authorization associated with the ID. Using the same process, if a door access report was requested, the security system made a list of the IDs in the report, and requested the names of the individuals accessing the doors from the downtown computer. The names, as they appeared in their personnel files, were then listed in the report.

Per industry standards, all databases used by a computer should be stored on that computer. The technique of looking up data on another computer as opposed to storing databases on a host computer was a flaw in the Desert Canyons security system. This one programming flaw was, however, deemed necessary because there were so many small, outlying facilities in the utility that keeping a satellite set of databases on each site would be cost-prohibitive and confusing. The security system had too many people with constantly changing authority levels on too many sites. A central lookup table was the most cost-efficient and workable answer. The defect in the logic that left the door access system vulnerable was that the utilities security team did not protect the lookup database at the home office with the same degree of security as they did the door security systems at the various facilities.

There was yet another flaw in the on-site door access system. The door security systems at the various facilities didn't check to see if the requestor had ever entered the room that they were now attempting to leave. This protocol was an artifact of the utility mindset when all the facilities were small and uncomplicated.

While the on-site security system was protected, the downtown central personnel computer was wide open and undefended. By changing selected ID numbers in the central personnel computer, Manuel could authorize and cover up any access he wished, for anyone he wished, at any time he wished. He was aware that his changes had been noticed and that the problem was being blamed on the on-site computer. So far, Manuel was in the clear.

Chapter Two

Sing had not always been the family name. Grandpa Singh was born Omran Singh in the Khambhat River delta region of western India. It was popular family lore that before Omran, the family had been Jats (peasants) in the Indian state of Uttar. They had been a small family of goat herders. At some point in the past, the Singhs moved, en mass, to Muslim-dominated Khambhat, to escape political and religious discontent. In Khambhat, the family opened and operated a building materials supply and contracting business. In good times, there was a steady need for stone, brick, concrete, and skilled artisans. The Singh family was moderately successful and content.

By the 1930s, Omran had assumed leadership of the family and operating control of the building supply business. It was also apparent to Omran that the Muslim influence was losing ground in the area. The rising influence of the new giant, China, also weighed heavy on his mind. In his quiet moments, Omran looked away to potential new homes.

India's close political connection to the British Empire made England a particularly attractive option, but England was heavily populated and didn't have the most dynamic economy. England was, however, tolerant of ethnic and religious differrences. The trump card was the economy: the family had to have a means of making a living. Expanding a construction-oriented business would be a long and complicated process in England.

Australia was another option. It was a booming frontier country with unlimited growth potential, however, emigration to Australia was tightly regulated. Racial background was almost as prejudicially regulated as it was in South Africa. It was unspoken, but it was there. He felt that a minority-owned family business would struggle too much in Australia.

The Emirates of North Africa had booming economies with unlimited construction potential and were predominantly Muslim, to the point of oppressing all other religions. North Africa, however, had other negative characteristics. The government tightly regulated foreign influence of any kind. Citizens in good standing with the current regime were the select few who had a fair chance at commercial success. Even then, anyone who was not related to the current royal family was relegated to being servants, laborers, and employees.

Then, there was the United States: huge infrastructure building projects (roads, dams, airports, etc.) were everywhere and population was low. Commercial potential was highest in the U.S. The Muslim religion wasn't dominant, and religious freedom was a building block of the U.S. Constitution. The family could blend in and worship as they wished. There was a lot of racial tension in the news, but it was focused on the African-American population. Minority races and religions seemed to be able to carry a low profile and assimilate into the population with minimal difficulty. The difficulty with the U.S. was getting into the country and staying in the country. The U.S. tended to limit immigration to the classifications of people that the U.S. needed (doctors, engineers, artists, teachers, and the like); people who wouldn't be a burden on the country's impressive resources. The U.S. was Omran's choice. Now, the Singh family needed a plan.

After several family meetings, the family decided that Omran and his wife would be the first to make the daunting move to the U.S. and open Singh Building Materials in California. Omran's two brothers would take the helm of the India-based arm of the business and would syphon as much operating capital as possible to Omran's growing branch in the States. As Singh Building Materials became successful enough to need more employees, the family would bring Omran's children and other family members to the U.S with guaranteed employment. In time, the family would close and sell the India branch and the last of the family would move to California. It was a good plan, and it worked.

California was economically generous to Singh Building Materials, and the Singh family did well. They weren't rich, but they were upper-middle class. In time, Omran changed Singh Building Materials to Sing Building Materials. The American-ized spelling of the family surname would be less controversial in the business community. He also adopted Western dress codes and traditions. He was an American now, an American of Indian ancestry, but an American. He wanted to retain one beneficial aspect of his family's heritage–

their national language, Hindi. True, English was an unofficial, secondary national language in India, but it was the family's fluency in Hindi that he wanted to preserve. He required everyone in his family to speak English when they were outside of their homes and Hindi when they were inside their homes without American visitors. It was his wish that as many members of the Sing family as possible be fluent in both languages.

He also recommended (demanded) that all the men in the Sing family serve in the American military. They were Americans, now. They had freedoms, and the obligations that came with those freedoms. The Sing family would exercise its freedom and obligation to civic duty to the U.S. by serving in the U.S. military.

Sing's decision to require all the Sing men to serve in the American military proved to be uncommonly wise. Omran's oldest son, Mark (originally Marwan Singh), served four years in the Army Corps of Engineers. Military schools opened new worlds of material science and construction techniques to Mark. He absorbed the knowledge like a sponge. After leaving the service,

Mark got his Material Sciences degree and a Master's in Business Management. As was his destiny, he assumed the leadership of the family business. Mark married a girl his parents chose. She was of suitable Indian status, well-educated, and American. They then started a new Sing generation (the first American generation) with the birth of their son.

Charles was born on December 11th in 1951. Charles served in the U.S. Navy before attending college. Brian's father also groomed Brian to take over the family business, but the pattern ended there. Charles selected his own wife, an American beauty of mixed ethnic backgrounds, named Abigail. She had the usual complement of English, Irish, Scottish, and German ancestors, but she also had a liberal Spanish, French-Canadian, and Native American (Choctaw from the Oklahoma Indian Territory) side to her. She had inherited the most attractive traits of all her ancestors. She was stunning, and her racial origins were ambiguous, at best. At twenty-three, Charles and Abigail had their first child, a son, of course.

Brian was born on his father's birthday, December 11th, in 1974. He inherited his father's sense of business and his mother's grace and beauty. He was taller than average, and thin. He also displayed an exotic aura of self-confidence that women noticed. Moreover, because of his diverse background, racial prejudice was as foreign to him as his right hand hating his left hand because the thumb was on the wrong side. He grew up just being *Brian*.

Brian excelled in school. He seldom brought homework home and just seemed to already know most of his lessons. Charles had great hopes that Brian would follow the family tradition of firstborn sons taking over the business, but Brian had no interest in building materials or operating a family business. Computers and the new advances in nuclear power plants fascinated him. Brian had his own mind and chose a different direction for himself. On April 18th, 1992, Brian graduated from high school and joined the nearest U.S. Army ROTC program. He couldn't wait to go out and change the world.

Chapter Three

As the morning progressed, Brian slept and Lenell made phone calls to verify background information from work applications. Outside, at 11:30 a.m., there wasn't a cloud in the sky, not a breath of movement in the air. It was seventy-five degrees, and the day was perfect. The trees and grass in Independence City Park were springtime green, and the smell of fresh-cut grass was in the air. Even the open desert seemed to have a green tint to it. While most of the older kids were in school, a few mothers enjoyed the fresh spring air with their younger children. Children chattered, dogs played, and a trio of retired couples power-walked on the bike path next to the river.

Nearby, a man in an aging, four-door Volvo pulled into a parking place next to the last picnic table at the end of the park. Joseph stepped out of the Volvo, stretched, and smiled his biggest, most disarming smile. He surveyed the park. The picnic table he parked next to was a little isolated, but in complete view of the rest of the park. There was no playground equipment nearby. It was perfect. He retrieved the stained, wooden box containing the carved, ivory chess set, and picked up the ice chest from his back seat. He put the cooler on the ground next to the picnic table and took a seat facing the parking lot. As he was setting up the chess set, Manuel Rojas pulled in and parked next to Josef.

The occupant of the third car to arrive was the contract-scheduling programmer by the name of Alex James. In his other life, Alex was an operative sent to the U.S. by The Family for Josef to train and use on the Desert Canyons operation. Alex secured a position at Desert Canyons as a temporary scheduling specialist for the refueling outage. He was the inside man for this project. Alex parked a short distance away and walked to the picnic table.

As Alex walked to the table, Josef's longtime associate, Mierie Asaud, pulled in on his motorcycle and parked behind Alex. Josef knew little about Mierie. He thought Mierie might be from Egypt, but didn't know for sure. They had worked together on three other projects, and Mierie had participated on one more before they met. Josef and Mierie shared an equal level of terrorist expertise and Islamic fanaticism. They were an effective team. Mierie was the cell's front man. He would go to the area of a proposed operation and start the recruitment process. He would look for people with certain traits like talking too much, alcoholism, gambling problems, sexual vulnerabilities, or a simple dislike for management. Josef would come in later, plan the project, and supervise the day-to-day execution of the project. Josef was also the point of contact to The Family and handled the requests for money, materials, or operatives with certain skills. The Family trusted Josef: they used Mierie.

After a given project ended, Mierie was responsible for cleaning up any loose ends when it became necessary. Both Josef and Mierie knew that if too many people disappeared at the end of a project, the authorities would notice and might link them together. To keep from being noticed, post-project cleanup was often delayed by weeks or months. Josef suspected that the cleanup at the end of the project was Mierie's favorite diversion. He was obsessively efficient and had never left a clue. He was a ghost. He was a demon. Josef was glad that Mierie was on his side and held him in the highest esteem. But, he also feared

Mierie and was sure that, if ordered, Mierie would eliminate him as easily as he would put out a cigarette. Mierie was emotionless and cold. He had the soul and life force of a frozen, polished stone at the bottom of a dead sea.

Mierie set up another chess set, and everyone sat. Then, Josef opened the ice chest and handed out homemade sandwiches, bagged chips, three beer cans, and a coke for Manuel. No one reacted to the fact that the beer cans were open.

At twelve, as if on cue, the three Muslims bowed their heads and went silent. Rojas sat patiently. After a minute or two, Josef looked up and muttered something in Arabic.

As they prepared to eat, the men talked and laughed. They used American hand gestures to accent their chatter. Manuel moved some of the chess pieces to make the boards look like they were playing the games. A small terrier puppy ran by the table, hopping and gamboling with abandon. Two toddlers, squealing with delight, chased after the puppy.

"Good morning," the mother said as she passed.

"Good morning. Beautiful day." answered Josef with a smile. He gave the woman his full attention.

"Who's winning?" she asked, gesturing to the chess sets.

"It's too early to tell, but, from experience, I like to think it's me. Ha, ha."

The family moved on. Four old friends looked like they were playing chess at a picnic table in a park and would have made a perfect Norman Rockwell painting. The title of the painting, however, would have been, <u>The Cabal Meets</u>.

Josef and Mierie realized early on that they needed to be invisible. While this scene might seem obvious, Josef believed that even the smallest detail of dress, speech, action, or attitude might result in them being noticed. A couple of years earlier, Josef's best friend had been noticed, followed, investigated, detained, and spirited away to an undisclosed center for interrogation because of precisely this type of oversight. The instructors at the training camp had taught them how to protect a private conversation by lying down on the grass in a public park, on their stomachs, heads on their hands, face-to-face, a few inches apart. This made it difficult for anyone listening to overhear, much less record a conversation. The technique worked well. Eavesdropping on such a conversation was impossible, but the men participating in this style of conversation might as well have 'Islamic Trained Terrorist' tattooed on their foreheads. Nobody could overhear the conversation, but anyone with terrorist related training knew exactly *who* they were and exactly *what* they were doing.

Today, Josef had chosen a picnic table in a public park, not the stereotyped basement of work shed behind a rundown house. They hid their meetings in plain sight. A week ago Wednesday, plain sight was the horseshoe pits behind City Hall. Before that, they mingled with the revelers at a craft fair at the coliseum. They had flown kites and cheered the jet boat races. They blended.

How they looked was as important as where they met. Josef didn't allow military style haircuts, heavy beards, and combat boots. Josef coached his crew on proper facial expressions, grooming details, and on how to project an American image. They learned how to smile when a situation dictated. Josef also insisted that none of his crew look as though they 'just got off the boat.' For some of his new arrivals, the American look was difficult to achieve. Most of the time, Josef insisted on polo shirts, jeans, and loafers. When appropriate, however, the men might not wear socks or might add aviator sunglasses.

When they ate out, they didn't order Middle Eastern food or drinks, and they carried American cigarettes whether they smoked or not. Josef chastised them for the use of Near-Eastern hand gestures. Beyond simple waves, hand gestures didn't easily flow across cultural lines.

Alex James, like all novice operatives, found controlling his projected image challenging. Josef chastised cell members if they showed a negative facial or body reaction to any of America's over-indulgences. He also instituted his version of workplace sensitivity. Josef trained each operative to be gracious and submissive with women in positions of power. The hardest situation for most of them to master was staying passive when witnessing the constant barrage of news reports and discussions about America's continued criminal interference in Mid-Eastern affairs. Even when the cabal was alone in their living quarters, Josef required them to not react when television reporters related the latest acts of aggression and war as victories for democracy by the benevolent American government. They worked hard to appear impassive when overhearing that day's political discussions by average American citizens, but they did it. They blended.

Josef and Mierie practiced what Josef preached. They were adept at their camouflage. Josef was never concerned for Mierie or himself. The fact that they were participating in their fifth operation was testament to their skill.

Manuel was also adept at covering his true political and work-place opinions. While he was something of a loner, he didn't display too much rancor when criticizing management's stupid, self-serving decisions. Manuel blended in at the office, as well as Josef, and Mierie blended in everywhere else.

Alex James, however, was another story. The Son of the Lion was…unpredictable. He looked the part of a third generation Arab-American, but Alex's problem was that he couldn't cover his involuntary reactions, even when he was alone (or thought he was alone). Veins popped in his neck at news stories. He would clench his fists at blasphemous religious discussions and hated interacting with women of authority to the point of feeling nauseated. It challenged his every fiber not to berate these women and force them to return to their proper place in the home, under the inspired guidance of a man. After a lot of practice in similar situations, he could recover his demeanor without being noticed, but his rate of recovery this time didn't satisfy Josef. Alex wasn't aware of how much Josef noted his failings because Josef could cover his involuntary reactions. Josef had already decided not to allow Alex James (Adawi Aimur-Noor) to jeopardize this or any future operation. Josef's dilemma was that Alex was the central player in this operation. Alex walked a fine line and, by necessity, so did Josef.

While Josef changed many aspects of his life and his displays of faith to blend into American culture, he was not willing to compromise his dedication to his faith. For these few, hardened rules of life, Josef disguised his preferences to fit the culture around him. One such incorruptible aspect of Josef's faith was Islam's ban on drinking alcoholic beverages. Joseph pre-filled the beer cans with a dark, Moroccan mint tea popular with North African Muslims. He had poured the beer down a drain at his apartment, washed the cans, and refilled them with tea. He also refused to work with a Muslim who broke the Islamic covenant against the consumption of alcohol. However, he had no objection to appearing to enjoy an occasional drink. Anyone observing the scene would see men of possibly Arabic descent drinking beer and playing chess. Fundamentalist Islamic terrorists didn't idle their time away playing games or drinking beer.

The forced compromise that gave Josef the most concern was his beloved call to prayer. One of Josef's earliest and most profound childhood memories was hearing (or sometimes waking to) the morning Adhan for the predawn prayers. Waking to the call to prayer was comforting to Josef's soul. The beautiful voice washed over him and cleansed him of his fears and insecurities. It reassured him that Islam and Allah were there for him, would always be there for him. He felt empowered knowing that Muslims everywhere were hearing and responding the same as he was. Josef knew that, in Allah's eyes, he was as good as any other true believer. While kneeling in prayer facing Mecca, he knew he was a part of something larger than himself, something larger than life. He felt connected and needed. After all, the experienced, learned men around him couldn't all be wrong. There was an order woven into the world around him, and he fit into the fabric.

During Josef's time in the Western world, he heard no comforting call to Morning Prayer in the air around him, but he could still hear the call as his clearest and most vivid memory. Josef coordinated his day so that he was always sitting down to a meal that world require the saying of grace. He would bow his head, mentally face Mecca, mentally touch his forehead to the prayer rug, and mentally avow his prayers. He would remember. He would remember Islam, and he would remember why he was here.

For now, however, it was time to work for the glory of Allah. He picked up a sandwich, took a bite, and moved one of the larger chess pieces on the board. Too bad Josef didn't actually play chess. He turned his attention to today's task.

Chapter Four

"Alex, how did the rehearsal go last night?" asked Josef. "Did everything time out correctly? Were there any glitches, any problems, anything unexpected?"

"All went well," Alex said. "A couple of people saw me without seeing me, as you said they would. The expired badges functioned as expected. The computer granted me access to selected doors as expected. No one challenged my movements, as expected." Alex sat up straighter and moved a chess piece, but didn't mention seeing Brian Sing.

"And you, Mr. Rojas, any response to your accessing and changing ID numbers?" Josef asked.

"It all went off like clockwork. After the morning request for a door access report from Lenell Spector, I restored all the ID numbers to their originals. Our four badges are expired and anonymous, once more."

"I am getting concerned that Ms. Spector may not be buying the idea of a programming error in the site software as the reason for the extra access entries. She requests more reports than anyone else," Manuel noted as he executed a 'ta-da' hand gesture over the chess set in front of him.

"Other than the electronic r-quests for access reports, has Ms. Spector made any other inquiries? Has she asked questions through any other media, e-mails, IMs? Has she raised any questions during any meetings?" Josef asked.

"No, not that I know of," admitted Manuel.

"She hasn't noticed anything," Josef said matter-of-factly. "Requesting reports is part of her job. She assumed these extra door open requests are a bug in the on-site system, as I said she would. If she ever does anything beyond requesting these morning reports, you contact me. Otherwise, let it go," Josef shrugged, but made a mental note to remind his hacker group to be extra vigilant in monitoring Ms. Spector's communication.

Manuel nodded.

"Okay, any other questions or observations?" Josef asked. He smiled his *concerned father* smile as he searched the eyes of the other three men for signs of disagreement. In a single motion, he scanned the area around them. Then he moved another chess piece and leaned toward Rojas expectantly.

Manuel jumped slightly as he remembered his role and moved a chess piece.

"No? Then it is time to go through the script once again. Tell me, step-by-step, how we will destroy the Desert Canyons Nuclear Power Station on May 1st and contaminate half of Southern California in the process. Praise be to Allah. Who starts?"

"I do," answered Alex. "I will set my alarm and wake at 4:10 a.m. I will shower and dress in cargo pants, polo shirt and cargo vest. I will put the four stolen ID badges, marked A, B, C, and D, into individual metal foil envelopes to prevent detection by the electronic security scanners and put them in my upper left vest pocket."

Manuel spoke next, "I will set my alarm to wake me at 4:00 a.m. I will eat and get dressed as usual. My wife will not wake up with me."

"I will leave my apartment at 4:48 a.m.," recited Alex.

Manuel added, "At 4:55, I will leave for the office."

Alex continued, "I will go through Canyon Lakes Vehicle Security Gate and park in the employee parking lot before 5:05. I will wait to enter the admin building until 5:05, with the rest of the early birds on the shutdown crew. I will have one hour to retrieve the key and assemble my tools in my cargo pockets."

"Stop," commanded Josef. He clenched his jaw as he stared at the chess set before him. In a strained, controlled voice, he emphasized, "You must be precise! You must be precise! You will not have 'one hour.' You must get your key and your tools and be ready to leave the common areas at 6:05…at 6:05…not in an hour! If you arrive at the Turbine Building door too early or too late, Manuel will not have the correct ID codes in place. ID A would cause an 'Unauthorized Access Request' alarm in the control room. Please, be precise." Josef called upon all his discipline to maintain the remnants of his even demeanor. True, this was a practice/training exercise. Mistakes made here brought a stern correction. The same mistakes made during the operation would be disas-trous.

"Continue now, Alex. You will assemble your key and tools, and then…" Josef noticed a small fishing boat leisurely trolling up the river in front of the park. The anglers never looked toward them.

"I will assemble my key, tube of epoxy and tools in my pockets and be prepared to leave the employee common areas at 6:05." Alex recited with an apology in his voice.

Alex recited. "The key is stuck to the back of a structural beam with double-sided tape in the farthest corner of the lunchroom from the doors. It is six inches above eye level on the back of a support beam where no one would stumble across it. I will collect two ¾ inch box wrenches, a cable splitter, a small electronics tool kit, and a dozen #18 wire splice nuts from the various desk drawers in the student intern office."

The utility company assigned as many student interns from the local colleges and high schools to the various site offices during special operations as possible with the objective of assigning minimum duties to the students while providing maximum exposure to the plant operations. Some of the students earned minimum wage. Others exchanged work for grades. During the outage, when interns had a break from their mentors, they would retreat to the temporary intern office. The intern office (a commandeered conference room) had a dozen desks, a dozen computers, a printer, and a copier. On most days, they worked on menial computer assignments. Like most young adults of dating age, they talked, laughed, and flirted amongst themselves. None had any possessions or office supplies. No one used the desk drawers, so no one noticed two wrenches in the bottom drawer of one desk, or the handful of wire nuts in the pencil tray of another. Alex had placed the items, a few at a time, in the drawers. On the day of the operation, Alex was to collect all the items.

Manuel spoke next, "I will arrive at my building downtown at 5:15 and mix with the staff coming in early to support the outage. I will go to work as usual, and make certain as many people as possible see me. I will continue my normal, boring routine until 6:12."

"No need for extra editorial words or remarks, Mr. Rojas," chided Josef as he illegally moved a pawn.

Mierie spoke for the first time, "I will be up by 6:00 a.m., dressed and ready. I will check our websites for random inquiries to any of our participants." He moved a chess piece and took a drink of tea.

On cue, Alex said, "At 6:13, I will leave the common areas and walk to Turbine Building door TD-6. I will arrive at 6:15."

"Thank you for being precise, Alex," said Josef. "We can't leave the incorrect ID numbers in place too long. Some other computer system might try to access the correct number while we have the incorrect number in place. We don't want the payroll computers reporting that Chief Operations Supervisor Brown no longer works for the utility, do we? Continue."

Manuel was next, "At 6:12, I will access the personal access records for the people whose badges we have, and raise the first digit to a nine. No computer will search for a number that high, and we won't have two search results on one ID during the operation. Then, I will access the personnel record for Chief Operating Superintendent Thomas Brown and enter the ID number from ID badge A. When the site access control computer searches for the ID number on badge A, it will find that the ID number belongs to an employee named Thomas Brown. The site access control computer will verify that Thomas Brown has door access authority for door TD-6 and open the door."

Alex continued, "At 6:15, I will enter the Turbine Building through door TD-6. While in the Turbine Building, I will retrieve the phone-triggered control box from the salvaged electronics storage shelves in the truck high bay."

The truck high bay was an interesting industrial space: four times as wide and three times as long as a single-trailer semi-truck. Access to the bay from the outside was via a two-story, extra-wide, roll-up, metal door. A skilled semi-truck driver could easily back a full-sized truck into the bay. The roof over the front half of the high bay was two stories tall and had an industrial, rail-mounted, full-range-traversing, overhead crane. The back half of the high bay was open to the roof of the main turbine deck at the top of the Turbine Building and to all six stories in between. Maintenance personnel removed or installed sections of the intermediate floors to create a variety of crane pit configurations. A driver would back a truck loaded with a large piece of equipment into the high bay. An operator would use the high bay crane to take the equipment from the truck, move it to the back of the high bay under the crane pit, and set down on the floor. After the operator moved the high bay crane out of the way, the operator of the turbine deck crane, high overhead, would use the turbine deck crane to lift the equipment to an elevation a few feet above the destination floor. After the destination floor was re-installed, the operator of the turbine deck crane would lower the equipment to the floor. Local cranes would finish the move. Most of the time, the high bay was little more than wasted space, but it was essential to moving heavy equipment in and out of the facility. For most of the operating year, all the floors were in always in place, and the high bay was a lot of empty space. As a result, the cabinets and shelves that lined the walls of the high bay contained a multitude of forgotten documents, unused spare parts, specialized electronic equipment, and mechanical paraphernalia. Alex's small box, with its exposed wires, could go unnoticed on these shelves indefinitely. In fact, as long as there was a thick layer of dust on it, a functional nuclear weapon could sit on the shelves for years without notice. Josef built the phone-triggered remote box weeks earlier, and one late evening that same week, Mierie dropped it on the riverbank inside the plant fences during one of his fishing trips. Alex then moved the box to the high bay shelves.

Manuel spoke next, "I will monitor the door authorization computer requests. When I see a request for authorization for ID A to open TB-6, I will restore Chief Operating Superintendent Thomas Brown's assigned personnel ID number."

Mierie suddenly broke everyone's concentration by laughing aloud and saying, "It was the funniest thing I've ever seen." No one looked at Mierie or reacted to the statement.

The four men sat in a modified square formation at the picnic table. Each faced the man on the far corner across from him. Even while reciting the script, each man also looked over the opposite man's shoulders for anyone approaching him, looking at them, or taking too much interest in them.

Mierie noticed that one of the elderly couples that had been walking on the path had now veered off and headed across the grass toward the parking lot. Their path would bring them close to Josef's picnic table.

Mierie's comment was a rehearsed signal to the others to change the subject of conversation.

Mierie continued, "The younger brother's wife, Daphne, on the television show Frazier, had gained a lot of weight. She had fallen to the floor and couldn't get up." He feigned a snicker, "Niles is painfully out of condition. He couldn't help her up." Guffaw. "Frasier was having back problems and he couldn't help her up. Marty, the father, is crippled and couldn't help her up." Mierie rolled his eyes. "So, all three men work together to help her up. Then Niles says, 'Maybe you've gained some weight, Daphne. It just took three Cranes to lift you off the floor'." The four men laughed over the situational comedy for several seconds.

While this break in the script took place, Josef's mind wandered as he reevaluated his decision to work without any written or drawn records of any kind for the project. The men committed every thought and action of the script to memory. In the beginning, the crew memorized the sequence of the first few actions. As they added new steps, they mentally edited the script. It started weeks ago. With no record but in the memories of these four men, there was no physical evidence that might incriminate them. Josef allowed no computer files, no thumb drives, no notebooks, and no paper copies. No paper or electronic trail meant no provable conspiracy. The favorite American buzz phrase, "he acted alone," would be the convenient explanation. The FBI could arrest them right now, and there would be no evidence to hold them or tie them together.

Thus, the script had been repeated dozens of times. It had been modified and refined. Everyone worked with the script without mistakes-- except Alex. He continued to have minor difficulties, which caused Josef to interpret Alex's continued lapses as a lack of dedication. Even with some mistakes, this was the primary training technique that Josef practiced.

Josef signaled a return to work, because he could best judge when the intruders were a safe distance away. Josef extended his hand, palm down, over the middle of the table. Without changing facial expressions or body language, the men switched back to the script.

Manuel spoke, "At 6:33, I will change Minerva Hopkins's personnel ID number to match ID-B." Minerva was the day shift Quality Assurance/ Quality Control inspector. Her job was to wander the facility, randomly comparing the details of recent QA/ QC reports with the real equipment in the plant. A record of her roaming the plant would raise no concerns.

Mierie interjected, "At 6:35, I leave my apartment complex with my fishing boat in tow and drive to the boat launch ramp."

Alex added, "Also at 6:35, I enter the Penetration Access Hallway of the containment penetration building through door PSB-34."

The Containment Vessel is the big domed building that is so highly visible to the public at most commercial nuclear power plants. It has two primary functions. First, the power plant's designers placed a majority of plant equipment that processed contaminated materials in the Containment Vessel. Second, the Containment Vessel contained all the contaminated fuel byproducts if they escaped the integrity of the nuclear fuel, as it was at Chernobyl. However, the Containment Vessel for the Chernobyl Nuclear Power Plant was open for a refueling operation at the time of the Ukraine accident.

The penetration support building surrounds the outside of the Containment Vessel on the ground floor and first basement level. The penetration support building is little more than a ring of small rooms that each share a wall with the Containment Vessel. Because of the proximity of these rooms to the Containment Vessel and the reactor just inside the Containment Vessel wall, the radiation levels in these rooms were dangerously high for people. When the plant design calls for a pipe or cable to run from outside the Containment Vessel to inside the Containment Vessel (or vice versa), the pipe or cable runs to a penetration room. The pipe or cable, along with dozens of other pipes and cables, routes around the penetration room to the appropriated containment vessel penetration. As one would expect, the containment vessel penetrations are the weak points in the Containment Vessel. A hallway runs around the outside of the penetration rooms for access. Due to the high radiation levels in most of the penetration rooms, people avoided entering the hall or the rooms without a specific purpose, and they didn't stay long. While the radiation levels in the penetration rooms were not high enough to kill the unwary, they were high enough to give a person a noticeable case of radiation sickness if he or she stayed in one of the rooms a half an hour or more.

One penetration room in the northwest corner contained a personnel hatch. It had pneumatic outer and inner doors with a pressure chamber between them like a deep-sea diving habitat. People didn't use this hatch often. A two-story equipment hatch was in a penetration room in the southeast corner. It was twelve feet across, concave against inside pressure, and always bolted shut during operation.

Again, Manuel had the next action, "I will monitor the door authorization computer requests. When I see a request for authorization for ID B to open door PSB-34, I will restore the ID number for Minerva Hopkins."

Alex continued, "I will walk around the Penetration Access Hallway to room CM-24. Each room has one door and no windows."

Manuel said, "At 6:38, I will change Callum Holman's ID number to match ID-C." Callum was the shift Radiation/Contamination, or RadCon, Technician. He was one of the few people at Desert Canyons who could enter the Penetration Access Hallway and/or a penetration room and enter a medium background radiation field without raising a question.

Alex said, "At 6:40, I will enter Cable Penetration Room 24 through door CPR-24 using ID-C. I will have 30 minutes to install the remote trigger box."

Manuel said, "When I see the request for access to CPR-24, I will restore Callum Holman's ID number. Even though Alex will be in the room for a scant 30 minutes, we don't want an overachieving computer tech to trip over our bogus entry."

The remote trigger box was simplicity in the truest sense. There was a portable plant phone inside with a thirty-foot connection cable to connect to the computer/phone jack in room CPR-24. There was a phone jack in every room in the plant.

On the other side of the box was a bundle of individual wires with connection clips on the ends. Once in room CPR-24, Alex will locate two cables in one of the cable trays and strip off the outside insulation to expose the wire bundle inside. One wire in each cable was a ground, and another was a twenty-four-volt DC power supply. The remaining wires provided control and indicator feeds to the operator in the control room for the Primary Coolant Relief Valves. Alex would connect the ground and power wires from the trigger box to the power and ground wires in the cables and then connect the rest of the wire clips to designated wires in the cable bundle. Installation time for the remote trigger box was about twenty minutes.

Once connected, the remote trigger box controlled two of the three solenoid-operated air valves for two of the three air operated Reactor Coolant Relief Valves. The wiring for the two valves entered containment through Cable Penetration Room 24. The third set entered the Containment Vessel on the far side of the building. The wiring for all the valves didn't go through the same room or cable tray, so no single event could disable all three air solenoid valves or Reactor Coolant Relief Valves at one time. The reactor coolant system collected heat from the nuclear reactor and transferred it up to water in the steam generators, like the cooling water system in an automobile.

The steam generators would then use the heat to make steam to drive the turbines.

Just like a car coolant system, the reactor coolant system had automatic relief valves to protect the system from too much pressure. Desert Canyons used compressed air as a failsafe feature to keep the relief valves closed. If the compressed air system failed, the Reactor Coolant Relief Valves would open to a safe condition, thus protecting the reactor's coolant system. Electrically operated air solenoid valves would control the air to relief valves. The solenoid valves energized open to admit the compressed air, then de-energized to vent the compressed air. If the plant's electricity failed, the air valves would close, removing the compressed air supply. The remainning compressed air would then bleed from the relief valve's air control cylinders and, as before, the relief valves would open. If the pressure got too high in the reactor, electronic relays would remove the electric power from the air solenoid valves and the relief valves would open.

Each air solenoid valve and Reactor Coolant Relief Valve had several position switches mounted on it. Different switches closed for different valve positions: open, closed, not open, not closed, and (rarely) somewhere in between. Some of the position switches controlled small indicator lights and computer inputs so the operators in the control room could monitor the current position of the different valves. The control room operator also had a button available on the main control console that he could push to de-energize the air solenoid valves.

For Alex, the connections for the remote box were simple: he had practiced the connection procedure until he could do it in his sleep. If the downloaded wiring diagrams were correct, he would have no problem.

Alex would remove the outer insulation and cladding from the two cables that controlled the A and C relief valves, exposing the individual wire bundles. Then, he would remove t-he insulation from one of the ground wires from one of the cable bundles and connect the trigger box ground clip to it. Next, he would remove the insulation from the power lead from one of the cable bundles, without cutting the wire, and then connect the power lead from the trigger box to the exposed power lead from one of the cable bundles.

Once power and ground were established, Alex would cut the wire for each control room indicator light that should be lit during normal operation, then clip a 24VDC wire to it. This done, the normal array of operating indicator lights would stay lit no matter what happened to the valves. In the control room, the valve position lights would indicate that the valves were in their normal position. With a scheduled outage starting in two hours, there would be enough chaos in the control room that no one would notice the momentary blink of the valve position indicator lights as Alex connected the wires.

Alex would then simply cut the wires for the remaining position indicator lights that were dark during normal operations. These particular indicator lights would then never illuminate. The result of the rewiring would be that the position indicator lights for the A and C Primary Coolant Relief Valves would show a normal, but incorrect, operating condition, indefinitely.

Alex wasn't going to touch the computer inputs, which would report changes in operating status far too quickly for manual wiring changes. Besides, a discrepancy between the computers reported valve position and an indicator light would add to the general confusion during the 'accident.' The control room valve position indicator lights, considered the most reliable source of position information, would show normal operating positions as the reactor self-destructed.

Next, Alex would connect the cut wire stubs coming from the position switches to lights on the control box that would then show the correct air solenoid and relief valve position. At that point, no one but Alex would know the true valve positions.

Alex's next move would be to connect normally closed contacts on an electric relay in the trigger box to the two air solenoid valves. During this step, the valve would close momentarily, and then reopen. The position indicator light on the control box would go dark for a few milliseconds and then re-illuminate. He'd know he had control of the correct valve when the indicator light flickered. The control air wouldn't have time to bleed away. The relief valves wouldn't open until Alex activated the trigger box to open the valves.

Alex's final step would be to connect the communication cable from the trigger box to any computer/ phone jack inside the penetration room. If Alex called the number from any phone, inside the plant or out, the computer would search all phone connections in the plant and then connect the call.

The operators at the power plant were excited when engineering installed this innovative technology. There was too much electronic and noise interference for radios or walkie-talkies to work properly. There was too much noise in other areas for PA or broadcast communication to be reliable. Josef liked the communications upgrade, as well. With this technology, an operator could simply plug in a phone to any phone jack and call any phone in the facility.

For Alex's purposes, when he called the phone number, the computer would connect the call, the ringer would energize the trigger box relays, and the normally closed contacts on the relays would open. The air solenoid valves would close, and the

Reactor Coolant Relief Valves would then open. The control box was an elegantly simple instrument of mass destruction.

The trigger box had one more feature: it contained two pounds of magnesium-based fuel/air incendiary material. Thirty seconds after the trigger initiated, the control box would expose the incendiary material to the air, and it would ignite. This metal-based material burns hotter than a blowtorch, hotter than a cutting torch. The resulting fire would consume the aluminum box and vaporize most of the contents. The fire would also consume a large section of the nearby cables, cable trays, and structural materials. It might even destroy the integrity of one or two of the containment penetrations themselves. More holes in the containment wall meant more nuclear waste venting to the outside world.

Without pause, Mierie said, "I will arrive at the boat launch at 7:00, launch my fishing boat, and wait."

Josef turned to see the mother, two children, and their dog heading for their car as Manuel said, "At 7:08, I will change Callum Holman's personnel ID number to match ID C."

The men recited their steps with more staccato now. Josef took a second can of mint tea from his cooler and moved a chess piece.

Alex said, "I will make sure that I take all spare tools and parts with me in the pockets of my cargo pants. At 7:10, I will exit room CPR-24. Then, I will go to door CPR-32, and enter Pipe Penetration Room 32."

"I will go to the northwest corner of the room, to Containment Sump Blowdown Valve, BD-127. I will use key CCH-127 to open the lock on the 'No Access' box that covers the manual handle for the valve. I will use the two wrenches to remove the mechanical restraint on the valve and open it. I will replace the mechanical restraint and hammer the bolts with the wrenches until it is impossible to remove them. I'll replace the valve handle cover lock, and then squirt some of the epoxy into the lock. I'll take all the extra tools and parts with me in the pockets of my cargo pants. At 7:18, I will exit room CPR-32."

Manuel spoke next, "When I see the second access request for door CPR-32, I will restore Callum Holman's ID number, then change the ID number for Linda Chow to ID C."

Linda Chow was a documents clerk in the payroll office downtown. She didn't have access authority to any doors at Desert Canyons. After the 'accident' is initiated, the first couple of computer reports would show that Linda Chow entered and exited rooms CPR-24 and CPR-32 while she was at home getting ready for work.

Manuel continued, "At 7:21, I will change the personnel ID of Minerva Hopkins to ID B."

Alex added, "At 7:23, I will exit the Penetration Access Hallway."

Manuel added, "I will monitor the door authorization computer requests. When I see an authorization request from ID B to open door PSB-34, I will restore the ID number for Minerva Hopkins. I will change the personnel ID number for George Tellico to ID B." George Tellico was the senior manager for employee benefits. "He doesn't have authority to access this door. Not only is he not at the plant, he's at a commercial insurance seminar in Washington, D.C."

Manuel continued, "At 7:29, I will again access the personnel record for Chief Operating Superintendent Thomas Brown, and enter the ID number from our stolen ID badge A."

Alex continued, "At 7:31, I will exit the Turbine Building via the Maintenance Building door and walk to where the gun is hidden."

Manuel finished with, "I will monitor the door authorization computer requests. When I see a request for authorization for ID A to open door TB-6, I will restore Chief Operating Superintendent Thomas Brown's assigned personnel ID number. I will then change the personnel ID number for Paul Hastings to ID A." Paul Hastings was a level six security guard at the utility wind farm a hundred miles away.

Alex next said, "At 7:33, I will retrieve the gun from its hiding place and continue to walk to the River Water Pump House."

Manuel said, "At 7:36, I will access the personnel record for biologist Janie Wilson and enter the ID number from our stolen ID D."

Alex lowered his voice without realizing it, and said, "At 7:38, I will use ID D to enter the River Water Pump House, and kill any operators that should be there."

Manuel started to say, "At..." when Josef interrupted, "What do you mean by 'should,' Alex?"

Alex thought for a moment and said, "Well, their procedures say that there will be a floor operator at the River Water Pump House, and he should have the Contaminated Liquid Waste Discharge System operating. What if the operators aren't there or the system isn't operating? I know how to increase the blow down concentration to one hundred percent. I don't know which valves to open and/or close. I don't know how to program the rest of the blow down electronic controller."

After a couple of deep breaths to alleviate his exasperation, Josef said, "We were not able to acquire an operating manual for that system. As such, we chose the date and time of our operation to compensate for this gap in our information. Those two hours, from 6:00 a.m. to 8:00 a.m., on May 1st will be the last two operating shifts before the start of a refueling outage. By procedure, the operators will complete any task that they can prior to the outage shift. The operators will fill the demineralized water tanks. They will process all trash, radioactive and clean. By procedure, they will pump all building liquid collection sumps to the River Water Pump House Holding Tank. The normal setting for the Holding Tank Pump is to mix the low-level contaminated liquid waste with river water and discharged the solution back into the river. The Operations Shift Supervisor for this shift will be Downing. Downing always follows procedure. Always. We're counting on it. A floor operator or training floor operator will be at the pump house and the Contaminated Liquid Waste Discharge System will be operating. Believe it. Do you have any questions?"

While Josef waited for an answer, he thought to himself, *Of course, there are questions.* With an unknown like Operations Shift Supervisor Downing, there were always questions. Downing would follow procedures to the best of his abilities if he remembered them. Josef had faith in Downing.

Josef also had faith that Alex would perform all the steps of the procedure, as he had memorized them. Josef had no faith that Alex would be able to adapt to unexpected changes in the plan. Alex's last question supported this belief. "If no one is at the pump house, shoot holes in the bottom of the Liquid Waste Holding Tank and let the radioactive waste flow across the floor and out the door. There is always a path forward."

Josef had been disappointed on more than one occasion by the quality of the operatives that The Family had enlisted for him, but Alex was the worst. If, for some unforeseen reason, Josef and Mierie were unable to continue with the project, Josef was certain that Alex wouldn't be able to complete the project either, much less make changes to it. Some people had leadership training and natural skills, some didn't. Alex didn't.

Josef needed operatives with training like the soldiers of the American military. Everyone in the American military was a potential leader. If the enemy eliminates the designated leader, another capable, well-trained leader will step up and take over. Josef had combat experience with military units of the other kind. Eliminating the leader of an insufficiently trained military unit was like cutting the head off a chicken. The rest of the mindless body might run around in confused circles for several minutes. Josef didn't need another headless chicken. He needed well-trained and intelligent operatives.

Josef did, however, smile slightly at the thought that comparing Alex to a headless chicken was an insult to the headless chicken.

The other thought that crossed Josef's mind was the decision that he would make a minor change in the script. It would be a miracle if Alex were able to complete the script as memorized. Josef knew that he would not be able to *ad lib* if anything went wrong. When this operation was over, Alex would be more of a liability than an asset.

Manuel had already continued, "I will monitor the door authorization requests. When I see a request for authorization to open the door to the River Water Pump House, I will restore Biologist Janie Wilson's assigned personnel ID number. I will change Martha Thaxton's personnel number to ID D." Martha was on maternity leave. "I will watch for two computer report requests from any source. When I see two requests, I will know that we have created enough confusion in the computer reports. I will return all the correct ID numbers to the correct people, including our four stolen IDs."

Alex continued, "After I eliminate the operations personnel, I will unplug the electric rollup vehicle door and make sure that the security padlocks are in place. I will move the small electric forklift over to the personnel door (it opens out) and connect the forklift chains to its push rail. I will back the forklift up to put stress on the chains, set the brake, and turn off the key. Short of destroying the doors, there will be no way for the operating or security staff to enter the pump house from the land side."

"I will then open the tie breaker that connects the pump house to the main facility, thus isolating the pump house electrically. The small emergency generator will start and provide 48 hours of internal power. I will turn up the dial on the contaminated liquid waste discharge controller to one hundred percent to pump out pure radioactive sludge. To make our day complete, at 7:48, I will call the trigger phone number, starting the destructive cascade."

*****

The last steps were to happen in the control room. Another minor player in the control room had repeatedly assured Josef that Operations Shift Supervisor Downing would misinterpret the relief valve indicator lights and jump to the incorrect conclusions that his cherished procedures dictated. Downing would make the final mistakes that would destroy the reactor itself.

*****

Scram is the term used by nuclear power professionals to describe the emergency shutdown of the nuclear reactor the same way operators use the term *Turbine Trip* to designate a sudden shutdown of the main turbine-generator set. The *Automatic Scram Computer* shuts down the reactor by inserting the safety control rods if any one of a dozen operating conditions (pressure, temperature, reactivity level, etc.) drifts too far from normal. The *Automatic Scram Bypass Switch* allows the operator to bypass the automatic Scram function. Operators need the Scram Bypass Switch because the operating conditions of the reactor fluctuate erratically during startup and shutdown operations. Without a bypass switch, it would be almost impossible for an operator to perform a controlled startup or shutdown on a nuclear reactor. Once the reactor is at full power and stable, the operator places the Scram Bypass Switch in Auto, and the Automatic Scram circuit protects the reactor.

*****

Josef needed the *Automatic Scram Bypass Switch* to be in *Bypass* during the incident to prevent the reactor from automatically scramming. Part of the normal shutdown procedure would be to turn the switch to *Bypass*. Josef was sure that Downing would turn the switch early if he got nervous and didn't want the reactor to scram in the last minutes of his shift. In case Downing did not make the critical mistake, Josef had placed someone else in the control room who would. All that Josef's extra man needed at that critical moment was for Downing's focus to be elsewhere. There would be a lot of confusion to distract Downing. Without the protection of the automatic shutdown of the reactor, the cascading reactor meltdown would be set in motion.

The Reactor Coolant Relief Valves would open and release the reactor coolant into the Containment Vessel. The Reactor Emergency Scram circuits would not function. The reactor coolant would boil away, the reactor would self-destruct, and the physical turmoil of the destruction would mix the radioactive waste with the reactor coolant. The resulting sludge would then spew into containment. The slight pressure of the steam inside the Containment Vessel would push the sludge through the open Blowdown Valve and into the Dilution/Storage Tank in the River Water Pump House. The Dilution Discharge Pump would then spew the poisonous waste into the river. In the confusion of the apparent Loss of Coolant Accident, it could be hours before any of the operators realized that radioactive sludge was being released into the river.

Once the radioactive sludge hits the river, we have poisoned the river for hundreds of years. Ground water would become toxic, and irrigation would come to a standstill. All the land in the valley would be uninhabitable. The river would also carry the radioactive sludge to the sea and spread it in every direction, where it would then mix with the sands on the beaches and flow north with the motion of the currents. The radioactive contamination of Southern California would be complete, and the chaos, glorious chaos.

*****

Mierie spoke next, "Also at 7:48, I will leave the boat launch, go to a spot on the river near the pump house and pretend to be fishing. I will arrive at 8:00."

Alex said, "At 8:00, I will exit the pump house by the riverside observation deck door. I will fill the door locks with epoxy on my way out. I will then jump down to the waiting boat."

Mierie said with some boredom, "I will drop Alex at the Elm Street Park pier and go back to the boat ramp."

Alex's final words were, "I'll walk to the San Diego Rapid Transit station two blocks up Elm Street, retrieve my change of clothes from our black Honda, and change. I will take the RTS to San Diego, then take the next available train to San Francisco and return to the Middle East."

Mierie related his last step, "After I drop off Alex, I will return to the boat ramp and take the boat out of the water. I will take the boat to my apartment building and leave the boat and trailer in the back parking lot. I, too, will change into more appropriate clothes and take a taxi to LAX. I will take the 1:30 p.m. flight to Dallas and wait for instructions."

Josef said, "If all goes well, you will both be out of Los Angeles before the authorities realize that this was no accident and that they have been attacked."

Manuel related the last step of his script, "I will go back to my normal routine."

Josef was leaving after this meeting, before the festivities began.

Manuel asked one last question, "After the 'accident,' I'll be on my own here. I know that, at some point, you will notify me when it is safe for me to leave for my new life without making myself a suspect. What if someone gets onto me before you send me the 'leave now' code?"

Josef realized that Manuel was concerned that he would be left behind, so he answered with as much phony sincerity as he could, "We have set up dozens of web sites. The accepted practice of the FBI is to do some discrete background inquiries to gather information before contacting a potential suspect. They want to arm themselves with as many incriminating facts as possible before the first interview. When they make their first inquiries, they will register on our website monitoring software. If we detect such an inquiry, our website administrators will send you a 'leave now' bulletin board notice. It will say, 'You may have won a '**SPICY**' prize. To collect, go now.' The word 'spicy' will be a different font from all the other words. The second you see that notice, leave. You will be ahead of the authorities. We have left no evidence that you were involved. Even your work computers have no electronic signature that you accessed or changed anything. Trust me. You are as safe as you can be. They have not connected you to the anomalous door-open events over the past couple of months. By the evening of May 1st, they will be far too busy to look for you. Stay relaxed and continue to perform your routine. In a couple of months, you will be living the life of a rock star in the Caribbean. Are there any other questions or comments?"

No one moved. No one spoke. Josef ended the meeting with, "Okay, we go on May 1st. We won't meet or contact each other again. You may leave now." He looked away from them and started to repack his chess set and the remains of lunch.

He added, "Mierie, please stay a moment."

Manuel Rojas and Alex James packed up and left. They were both near exploding with excitement and righteous conviction. The events of the next few days would satisfy life-long obsessions for both men. Neither could think about anything else.

When they were gone, Josef turned to Mierie and said in a confidential tone reserved for his closest friends, "It went well today."

Mierie nodded. He knew that more was coming so he didn't speak.

Josef took his time to phrase his question with absolute clarity, "Mierie, I know that I shouldn't ask, but how did you get a control key into the lunchroom?"

Mierie stiffened imperceptibly. He had excellent self-control. Mierie acknowledged the red flag for one long, concerned moment. As on other operations, after Mierie did the preparation legwork, his job was to monitor the other members of the group. He followed the other team members in rotation, watched where they went, who they met, who they talked to, websites they visited, who they e-mailed, who they texted, and what they said. He looked for unusual contacts. He searched for any sign that one of the members might be working with the authorities or getting cold feet. He scrutinized every conversation. He listened for anyone who might ask the wrong question or seek the wrong information. From anyone else, Josef's inquiry was the wrong question, seeking the wrong information. If anyone else had asked, Mierie would focus his surveillance on the asker. Even the smallest inappropriate finding would result in Mierie recommending to Josef that the member might be a liability to the operation. Not a good thing.

But this was Josef. These two men had had too many successful operations together for Josef to raise such a question at all. However, if Josef had asked such a question in front of Alex or Manuel, there would be a problem. It might encourage them to ask related questions despite Josef's hard rule against asking questions when there was no "need to know." Mierie worded his answer in as non-threatening a manner as possible. He also chose words that would send a warning not to make the mistake again.

Mierie said, "Agha, I have forbidden such questions if you do not need to know the answer. The authorities can't force you to divulge information you don't have. For you, this once: there is a machinist in the machine shop who makes all Desert Canyon's replacement keys and who is afraid that I will share certain pictures of him. He has been married for thirty-five years and has twenty-eight years with the utility. His retirement is close. He knows that he will lose it all if pictures of him in a motel room, with a prostitute, using illegal drugs, were to be made public. He lives in fear and complies with my orders. Alex has verified that the key is there. I do my job well, Agha."

Mierie paused and waited, yet again. Again, he felt that there was more.

Josef made his next statement in a voice laced with regret, "Alex is making me nervous, and his mistakes are raising concerns with me."

Mierie added, "With me, as well."

A cloud of seriousness fell over Josef as he asked, "Mierie, do you still have the automatic pistol–the one with the extended clip and silencer?"

Mierie nodded.

Josef asked, "Is it still clean?"

Mierie nodded.

Josef straightened his posture, evened his tone, and said, "We're going to change the script. You will take this pistol with you on the operation. I have two boxes of large, heavy, industrial-sized bolt and nut sets in my car. You will take them with you, as well. Put the boxes of hardware in the bow of your boat. When Alex steps down from the pump house observation deck, tell him that I am aware of the potential problem. Tell him we have information that the authorities may be watching him. Instruct him to move to the bow of the boat and put the heavy hardware in his pockets. Tell him that if the authorities stop him, he is to claim that he is a simple hardware thief. He will have expensive, nuclear-grade tools and hardware to support his claim. Tell him that he is to take the Honda and drive to Las Vegas. He is to use the Gilbert Johnson documents and stay in Las Vegas until we contact him. He should be so distracted by the change in plans and the prospect of a few all expenses paid weeks in Las Vegas that he will go to the front of the boat without alarm. As soon as he has sealed his pockets, unload the full clip into him. He should sink like a stone with all the extra metal in his pockets. I want to be sure that no gasses ever build up in the body and bring it back to the surface, ever. Make sure every organ in his body has a hole in it. As you return to the boat ramp, disassemble the gun, and drop the pieces at different intervals in the river channel."

"Agha, will there be a need to send any misdirected information to American Intelligence?" asked Mierie.

Josef knew what Mierie was asking. If there was even the slightest hint that American law enforcement was onto their little operation, Josef could send a message containing misdirected information home using a communication method that has been compromised by the CIA, like landline phones or the U.S. mail. He often used different communications media to send harmless true information around the world. He then monitored Western intelligence circles to see if any action took place in the minutes or hours after. If the Western intelligence started monitoring The Family's operations, then a minimum flow of benign information would be transmitted through the media to keep the line open until they needed it. The Family could disseminate crafted false information across the channel leading Western intelligence away from a real operation. Both sides played a continual game of information misdirection. Each side hoped that it had the upper hand. Western intelligence analysts assured Western intelligence that some phone traffic was legitimate: some phone traffic was suspect. While Josef believed that Western Intelligence didn't act on all intercepted data, he assumed that he could not use all land lines, including payphones. Burner cellphones were a covert communication choice of both sides. Both sides still used the U.S. Mail and systems like e-mail. Western intelligence had not yet focused on the fringe dating or sex sites–too bizarre.

Mierie was asking if there was any chance that the American intelligence suspected this operation on any level. Did Mierie need to send American intelligence on a snipe hunt to protect the next few days?

"No, I find no indication that the Americans even know we're here. I will be uncomfortable being out of communications with you for the next few weeks," said Josef.

"I agree." Mierie said, "There seems to be no open chatter directed at us. I, too, will be uncomfortable being out of communication."

"Also, you may not be able to get past airport security after firing the gun. Gunshot residue will be all over you. You will drive to Las Vegas. Use the Gilbert Johnson documents. Wait there until notified.

Make sure you enjoy yourself. You've earned it."

They walked to Josef's car. Mierie took the heavy hardware and left. Josef loaded his chess set and lunch trash into his car and paused. He turned and looked at the small family park that he would never see again. He looked at the park that would soon be in the middle of one of America's most destructive industrial disasters of all time. It pleased his sense of irony that Alex James would forever be a part of it. He smiled a simple smile. Josef didn't realize that the lunch debris was one beer can short. He had been too focused on detailing the change of script to Mierie.

Chapter Five

Tuesday, May 1st, 2013, was going to be the most glorious day of Alex James's life. For the first time in his life, he was going to accomplish something spectacular for the glory of Islam. That day would fulfill his every fantasy. He would demonstrate his worth to Allah.

Alex was born in Egypt on March 12th, 1980. His birth name was Adawi Aimur-Noor Kuzbari (the Son of the Lion). 'Alex James' was the name that The Family assigned to him for the time he spent in the west.

His mother's birth name was Suhad Sawalha. Suhad must've been an active baby at night, and kept her mother and father from sleeping. Her name meant *insomnia* in Arabic.

Suhad had spent a carefree childhood in the small fishing city of Al Qusayr on the Red Sea in central Egypt. Her father had three groves of date palms and exported dates all around Egypt and the Red Sea. The city of Al Qusayr had been a trading center in ancient times because of its strategic location on a major trade route between Egypt and Jordan. It was also on one of the more popular pilgrimage routes to Mecca. Al

Qusayr had been an ideal place for a girl to grow up.

Life was good for Suhad. Her family, while not rich, were middle class. Suhad never went hungry and never slept on the streets, but her family didn't own a television or radio, either. Her family had some status in the small town.

However, the small town that she called home was *too small* for Suhad. She wanted more… a lot more. She wanted to live in a big city. She wanted excitement. She wanted a car, a red car. She wanted to be someone important, someone known. She knew her destiny was to be a great diplomat, a world-renowned politician, a rich businesswoman or, at the least, a famous artist. Suhad had stars in her eyes in a land where men expected women to stay home, run the household, and raise the children in silence.

As soon as she turned fifteen, Suhad 'reluctantly' agreed to her father's plan (a plan that she, herself, orchestrated with considerable care) for her to marry a promising young man (Talib Kuzbari) whom she had known for most of her life. As a child, she had snuck out at night to star gaze with him. As a teenager, she had spent many summer days working in the date palms with Talib. She knew him well. She knew how to talk to him and how to think for him. He believed that their fathers had arranged their marriage. He also believed that he was fortunate beyond reason that Suhad would become his wife.

Suhad's father wasn't as happy with the arrangement as an Islamic father might be. He wasn't unhappy with it, either. The boy was a fine boy, and he knew how strong-willed his daughter could be. The marriage was a good one. The one big fly in the ointment was he knew that, in reality, his daughter had arranged the match, not him. He was more concerned with what his male friends would think of him if they ever found out that he allowed his daughter to perform a duty that was, by Islamic custom, *his*.

Nonetheless, Suhad had decided. She married in spite of her father's self-absorption with his public image. Suhad and Talib moved into a small room in the back of his parents' house, and they began working seven days a week in the date orchards. Their room was stark, three by four meters, with cinder block walls that were water-washed with subdued pastel colors. A small window with no sash or glass provided a limited view of the orchards. There were two doors in the room. One opened to the inside to the rest of the house. The other door was unique because it opened to the outside at the side of the house. In this area of Egypt, it was unheard of for a second bedroom to have a door that opened to the outside. Suhad and Talib could come and go without the involvement of the rest of the family.

Over the next few months, Suhad put away tiny amounts of money for a future move to a bigger city. No one missed the small denomination coins, and it wasn't long before she found out that her husband had a distant relative who lived in the industrial town of Benha, halfway between the exotic cities of Cairo and Alexandria. The difference between Benha and Al Qusayr was that Benha had an industrial based economy with many more career opportunities. Suhad soon began letting her husband convince her that moving to Benha was in their best interests. The future of their family depended on it.

Talib found work in Benha as a hod carrier. A hod was a small wooden platform carried on the shoulders and balanced with the hands. The workers piled copious amounts of brick and concrete building materials on the hod. The hod carrier then carried the load into a construction site, up ladders and across the platforms to where the bricklayers and craftsmen were working. It was backbreaking work, but he was young and strong, and he thrived. He made a name for himself as a hard-working and reliable laborer and his job provided a regular income.

Suhad also found work and a reliable income in a textile processing plant in one of the fabric dying operations. The region was known for its brightly colored textiles and marketed those textiles all over North Africa. Her job was to remove the heavy materials from the dying vats and carry them to the drying yards. What made the work more trying was that the dying chemicals were harsh to the skin on Suhad's arms and hands. Her skin always had the aggravated look of a mild chemical burn. Chemical smells permeated her clothes and hair, and she could taste the chemicals in her mouth. Her eyes always burned as she carried the loads out of the building and into the fresh air. She knew that the harsh chemicals were having a negative effect on her health, but the pay was too good. She also knew that it was easier to *find* a better job when she already *had* a job.

The industrious couple worked hard and saved their money. It was not long before they, with the help of their family, were able to acquire a rich, fertile acre of farmland with a small, one-room building on it, on the outskirts of town. In the United States, the one-room hovel would be called a farm-labor apartment. It was small and basic as a prison cell, but it had all the necessities of life. It was their first home together, and they loved it.

Instead of growing a rotating crop on their land, like their neighbors, Suhad had her husband plant rosebushes. Manufacturers used the scented oils harvested from the rosebushes in perfumes and cosmetics. Perfumes and cosmetics were the next big growing industry in Benha, and Suhad planned to be right in the middle of the economic boom. It wasn't long before Suhad and her husband acquired a second acre adjacent to the first. They were now making more money from the roses than they were from their day jobs. Suhad was also becoming widely known throughout the rose oil distribution business. The owner of one of the larger rose oil exporters in the area had noticed her professionalism and business acumen. They were living the dream.

After work, on a cool evening in late August, 1979, Suhad stepped out the front door of the small apothecary shop on a backstreet in Benha. She was on her way home. She had forgotten about the sights and smells of the chemicals in her eyes and nose. She no longer noticed the rashes on her hands and arms. She had been working a lot of overtime in the last few weeks and had some extra money. Earlier, she purchased a loaf of sweetbread for her husband and some small chocolates for her two-year-old son. She had received some good news this day and wanted to make the evening a festive one. Suhad's last purchase was from a neighborhood apothecary. The pharmacist made the order by hand for Suhad. It was a small quantity of a locally processed opiate derivative that the locals used to alleviate pain. She had been having some back pain and nausea brought on by the heavy work. To Suhad, the greatest gift she could receive would be to take the pain away for a few hours. With her hijab in place and her packages in hand, Suhad started her evening walking commute to her rose farm outside of town.

Suhad was still in the downtown shopping area of Benha, and people filled the streets. She looked up and down the streets as she walked. She didn't want to run into one of the radical Imams that made it their duty to accost women who weren't in robes and veils or were away from their homes without a male escort. The Imams seemed convinced of their special level of righteousness before Allah, and that their reason to be alive was to be Allah's voice on Earth. It was their duty to speak, with the authority of Allah, with as much drama as possible. These men were intimidating to the point of instilling fear when they shouted and lectured at anyone who transgressed from the strictest interpretation of Mohammed's word (as they interpreted the word, of course). She didn't understand these men. Islam was such a beautiful religion that always spoke of love, peace, forgiveness, compassion, and family. The kind words of Mohammed always seemed so full of serenity and caring. Yet these men always seemed to be so full of anger and hate. She also didn't understand how all the other reasonable men on the streets could stand by silently and watch these ranting maniacs accost women on the street. She would never let another woman verbally assault her husband in this manner.

Suhad was almost out of the business districts and no Imam had accosted. She put thoughts of them out of her mind. This was a quiet time for Suhad, a time to reflect on the beauty and the peace she found in the Islam faith. It was a time to bask in the kind and gentle words of Mohammed as her husband discussed them with her. For her, there was neither hate nor anger in her religion. The next few blocks were a heartbeat of quiet contemplation of her personal relationship with Allah. Peace closed in around her.

She left the last of the business district behind her and was walking among small houses. Even the houses were becoming more spread out. She was close to home and there were farms all around her. She could smell the roses, the musty earth, and the farm manure. It brought back memories of her childhood home. She missed the smell of salt from the sea. Well, not entirely the salt, but the salty air mixed with the smell of dead fish and a hint of diesel oil. Home would always be an idealized place.

A burst of gunfire erupted somewhere far across the city. There were short bursts from a machine gun, then several single shots, and then quiet. It seemed that there were more and more of these small shooting skirmishes in Egypt as political and economic unrest grew more strained. There was interference from other countries; Russia, Britain, America, France, Iran, and Syria. They all seemed to want to have their fingers in Egypt's future. The close proximity of Israel also caused friction based on the differences of theology. Of course, the local warlords fought all of them. Everybody seemed to want to impose their own personal agenda (or interpretation of Islam) on everybody else, and willing to use guns to do it. Yes, the gunfire off in the distance had become a regular occurrence. The good thing about tonight was that no one was shooting at Suhad as she walked home.

As she walked the last few blocks, she thought back to the woman she had seen, by chance, earlier in the day, giving a speech in the square across from where she worked. The speaker was presenting a message of women's rights in Egypt. She wanted all women to stand up for women's rights, especially the rights to vote and to have more control over their own lives. The message resonated with Suhad and seemed so true. It was profound, obvious, and relevant to Suhad's new place in life. She wanted to hear more. She needed to hear more. Suhad wanted to be a part of something larger than herself, and Egypt's women's rights movement was rushing in to fill that void in her life.

As soon as Suhad stepped onto their small farm, she could see her husband hard at work in the rosebushes, pruning and harvesting as he went. Her heart swelled with pride whenever she saw him because he was the kind of man who could work all day hauling bricks and concrete and still have the heart to come home and work a full evening in the roses. Suhad's young son played in the homemade playpen at the end of the row. She called and waved to her husband before stepping into their home. She quickly put away her packages, changed into work clothes, made a small snack, and joined her husband in the roses.

"Rohi (dearest)," she called, "you work too hard. Come and eat." Suhad set out a small amount of lamb and vegetables. The sweetbreads would be for dinner, later.

"Habiti (my love)," he called, "welcome home. Your day was good, I hope." He hugged his wife. "And you're later than usual. I was beginning to worry. What do you have there? It's tantalizing. You spoil me."

"I had to do some shopping," she said. "Come, take a break, and sit for a moment, eat. I have some exciting news."

"One moment, Umri (sweetheart), I must change the irrigation."

As Suhad set their snacks out on a blanket, Talib walked to the head of the field to change the irrigation. He siphoned irrigation water for his field from a large canal that ran along the property line. He lifted the six-foot length of flexible pipe from where it was, breaking the siphon, and then stepped over to the next six rows. Pipe still in-hand, Talib then built a series of small dirt cofferdams that would distribute the water into the next six furrows. He then dropped a ten-foot length of rope down through the pipe. The rope had a round, knotted bundle of rags tied to the end of it. He dropped the end of the pipe with the rag bundle into the canal water and laid the other end in his furrows. When he pulled the rope through the pipe, the rags pulled the water from the canal through the pipe and started the siphon. He knew that he was stealing water from the irrigation system, but as long as there was enough water to go around, it wasn't worth the effort or the time for the irrigation company to try and enforce the rules. He and his neighbors had been irrigating their fields this way for decades. It took about 90 minutes to irrigate the full length of the six rows and then Talib had to move the pipe. So, once he started the irrigation cycle, it was off for a snack with Suhad.

Normally, he pruned and harvested in the other rows of roses while the irrigation flowed. After the snack, he would do two cycles of irrigation, then go in for dinner. After dinner, he would do another three rotations while everyone else was asleep. Since he couldn't work in the roses at night, he would start the siphon at the top of the field, walk to the bottom of the field, and lay down in the dry part of the field with his feet in a row that he was irrigating.

When the water reached his feet, he would wake up, walk to the head of the row, and start another rotation of irrigation. He had to do this ritual six nights a week to provide enough water for all the roses. Around midnight, he would put the siphon away, go into the house, and sleep the rest of the night with his family.

*****

When he got back to the blanket, he picked up his son, set him on his knee, and smiled at Suhad. "I, too, have some exciting news. Mine will just take a moment. Let me tell you first before the call to evening prayer," he said. His eyes were dancing, and his grin was playful. It was all he could do not to grasp Suhad's hands and kiss them with gushing excitement.

Suhad nodded. Good news from both of them made this a day to remember. When he didn't start speaking, she looked at him inquisitively.

"I have been promoted to foreman," he gushed in a rush. "From now on, I will have a crew of twelve working for me. I will no longer have to carry the hod except when we're shorthanded. It also means that I will travel from job to job with the company. I will no longer have to re-interview for each job. My pay will be steadier. The best of all, this will mean an increase in pay. I am part of the company now."

As Talib finished speaking, they heard the call to evening prayer in the distance. "This is wonderful," she whispered. "I'm so proud of you, habibie," she beamed at him as he handed the baby back and took his prayer rug a few steps away to begin his evening devotionals. Suhad took a sip of sweet tea and a bite of sugar cracker as she and her son watched her husband. An emotion, the undefinable combination of love, admiration, comfort, and awe, overwhelmed her like a brief waft of a warm breeze. People like these made a country great: family-oriented, a foundation of faith, devoted to each other and willing to work hard for what they wanted. They were grassroots. They were the strength and backbone of Egypt.

As evening prayers ended, her husband walked back toward them and said, "You had news today, also. Tell me about it."

"Do you remember me telling you about a gentleman named Hussein? He is the owner of Incense Oils International, the largest rose oil distillery and export company in Egypt? He suggested to me that he might have a place for me in his company in the purchasing department because of all my contacts with the rose farmers in the area. When I picked up our mail…Oh, that reminds me, there is a letter from your father. It's in the house. Anyway, I found a letter from Hussein's company asking me to call and schedule an interview. I think he wants to hire me. This opportunity means shorter hours and more pay for me as well." With a genuine sense of relief for her own health, she thought, *yes, and it means that I can get away from those horrible chemicals, as well.*

Between bites, he said, "Umri, this is wonderful! This is what you've always wanted, the opportunity you have been working for, an opportunity to work in the business side of the rose oil industry. Praise Allah. As always, I must ask, do you want me to call tomorrow and make the appointment for you? We don't want to risk offending the wrong traditionalist for such an important call. You know these people better than I do." he smiled as he handed his son a sliver of cheese.

"I can make the call." Suhad answered. She knew that her husband meant no insult. They often deferred to each other when the dictates of their culture and religion might cause a problem. Some men might take offense that a woman would call them on business. They each had their own skills and social place in the outside world. "I know everyone in I.O.I.'s front office."

"Go with my blessings, Sumaira (little princess). I can't wait to see how you will remake their world. Promise, though, that you won't forget me when you become rich and famous?" he added in mock desperation, rolling his eyes, and laying his head to one side. She knew that he was kidding and meant it as a statement of his belief that he knew that she would be wildly successful in her new opportunity. Both found comfort in the fact that Suhad believed in her soul that Talib completed her as a person.

So supportive, she thought, *it seems so natural for him to let me grow as he is growing.* "Today, we congratulate each other," she said, "If all works well, within a few months, we may be able to buy the additional two acres we talked about. We can consider having another baby. It is time for our family to grow."

"It is, indeed. It is, indeed. I must return to my work now. I'll come in in an hour or so for dinner, and we'll talk more," he said. Tonight, he would attack his tasks with an uncontainable enthusiasm. Every sacrifice was easier to make when there was good news and growth. He went back to work. The sun was down, and the evening prayers were over. Talib would work for another hour before the twilight deepened too far to see the roses.

Suhad took her young son, went into the house, and began preparing the evening meal. She warmed the sweetbreads and put extra spice on the lamb. For her, there was also a pomegranate, her favorite fruit, left over from a few days ago. She gave a chocolate to her son.

When all was prepared, she took the package of opiate out of her pocket and took a small amount of it. She washed it down with sweet tea and sat back to rest for a moment. She let the day drift away as she let go of the day, drifted, and rested.

Suhad rested as quiet as she could, letting her mind find peace, not knowing that, deep in her body, a small knot of cells was undergoing a frantic cycle of dividing, re-dividing, and growing. Each division was an individual step in a long, precise process that would result in the birth of Suhad's second son in a few months. By design, each division of cells would make perfect replicas of the original so the new baby would be healthy, but 'perfectly' didn't happen this night.

The whole DNA process is like building a long, high brick wall. If one brick in the bottom row is out of position, it's more difficult to maintain proper alignment of the bricks above it. By the time the top row of brick is in place, the one misaligned brick in the bottom of the wall will have made the whole wall weaker. Even if the mason compensates for the small misalignment by leveling the higher rows of bricks, there will always be a weakness in that section of the wall.

On this night, the accurate subdivision of cells was interrupted and misaligned several times. No one will ever know what caused this delicate process to go awry at that moment. It may have been a hormone out of balance with the rest of Suhad's body or a deficiency in Suhad's diet. It may have been the work chemicals or the small amount of opiate that she had taken minutes before. It may have been random chance, a cruel trick of fate, or time for that one-in-a-million misstep. Allah alone would be the one to know for sure.

That night, the small amount of opium created a small series of birth defects in another 'wall' of sorts. This wall would be the ventricular septum located in the heart, the wall between the left and right ventricles. Each flaw, if developed to maturity, would be called a membranous ventricular septum defect or a hole in the heart. A fully formed membranous ventricular septum defect would allow the blood to flow in the wrong direction through the septum with each heartbeat, resulting in a decrease of the blood flow to the body during the events when the body needed an increased blood supply the most.

In this unborn heart, no actual holes formed. Instead, the mutation of cells created a series of weaknesses in the ventricular septum of the heart. This heart would beat with predictable regularity if the child was calm and relaxed. The fibrous wall that separated the two ventricular chambers would function as designed. It would not bulge in either direction during a heartbeat and blood would flow normally.

But, if the child increased his activity level, the brain would call for more blood and an increase in blood pressure. The heart would beat harder and faster in response. The higher pressure would cause the rigid septum to bulge in the wrong direction with each squeeze of either ventricle, much like a water balloon bulged from any opening between the fingers when squeezed too hard. The fluttering bulge would then reduce the amount of blood pumped into the body with each beat of the heart.

If the body remained calm, the flaw would not force the septum forced to bulge into the ventricle. A calm life would mitigate or prevent the long-term damage. The ventricular septum might remain intact for a lifetime. However, if the septum bulged too often or too far due to stress, fear, or physical exertion, it would shred like a flag left to fly in high winds.

For Suhad, the evening passed in peace.

On March 12th, the next year, Suhad bore a second son. He was two weeks premature, smaller than she would have liked, sickly, and thin. Suhad, of course, loved him as only a mother could. He looked like his father, but, beneath the resemblance, Suhad noticed that he was frail. His hands and feet were too tiny. His cry sounded more like the weak cry of a kitten than the strong roar of a lion, and he seemed to tremble all of the time.

Suhad thanked Allah for the precious gift of their son. Yes, he might grow up to be small or frail, but he could have other gifts that would make him great. If Allah closed one door, He opened another. Her son would be a great talent or a noted scholar. Still, a little extra boost could not hurt. Suhad named her son Adawi Aimur-Noor Kuzbari (the Son of the Lion) for the fearless way he would live his life.

Suhad had no way of knowing that Adawi Aimur-Noor Kuzbari, alias the Son of the Lion, alias Alex James, would grow up to be a forgotten footnote in a lost 'top secret' file.

*****

As Adawi Aimur-Noor Kuzbari was taking his first weak breaths and crying his first pitiful cry in Egypt, halfway around the world in

California, Brian Sing was sitting down in front of the television to eat his favorite lunch. Brian was a robust five and a quarter years old, and growing out of his clothes like weeds overgrowing a garden. It was rare that his mother could get him to sit down to eat without the intervention of his father. He had too much energy, too many things to do, and too much in his imagination for him to sit down for a meal.

Today, Brian sat down on the couch, oblivious to the television. The two driving forces that dominated his life were, "how fast can I eat?" and "what adventures are Flash, Gordon, and I going to discover in the trees behind the house?' Flash and Gordon were the family pet Affenpinschers, a terrier-sized dog breed that originated in Germany. The name 'Affenpinschers' means 'monkey faces.' The breeder gave the breed that name because of its resemblance to a gorilla or chimpanzee. Brian believed the dogs were one of the more intelligent dog breeds in the kennel. Flash and Gordon were Brian's constant sidekicks. The three of them often ran the other two to the point of exhaustion.

Brian was inhaling his mac and cheese with sliced hotdogs as fast as he could until he glanced at the television. Then, as if someone had taken a picture, Brian paused, the next spoonful of mac and cheese poised halfway between the bowl and Brian's mouth. He didn't blink. He didn't move. There was a documentary about an electricity-producing nuclear power plant in Saint-Laurent, France on the TV. Several men were working on a bright, shiny, stainless-steel piece of equipment. Mirror-like steel pipes crisscrossed the background, and huge, shiny bolts held it all together. The tools the men used were enormous. The men were all dressed in bright yellow suits and gloves. They wore Scott Air Packs (the industrial equivalent of scuba tanks) and had all the cuffs and collars taped close around the arms and neck. The mac and cheese on Brian's spoon grew cold. Brian was a science fiction fanatic and followed the burgeoning Mars program with rapt interest. Brian could hardly comprehend what he was seeing. He always wanted to be a space man, an astronaut, or, at the very least, a firefighter, but five-year-old Brian knew that a world of space travel was still in the *far* future. *Star*

Trek: The Motion Picture came out the previous year, and Brian prayed that they would make more.

These men were working on the Saint-Laurent Nuclear Power Plant in France today… right now. The future for Brian, at five years old, seemed close enough to reach out and grasp. He lowered his spoon in slow motion and absorbed every picture and every word on TV for the next twenty minutes. There were giant cranes. There were special suits and the sounds of mechanical breathing. These men were repairing the reactor because some fuel rods had ruptured during a power surge. When the show was over, Brian ate his mac and cheese with sliced hotdogs without noticing that it was cold. He flew into the woods behind the house and lost himself for the rest of the day in the imaginary world of nuclear power plants. With his trusty crewmembers, Flash and Gordon, he worked miracles on the world's biggest nuclear power plant, saving the world and vanquishing alien invaders. Brian Sing, the boy with 'the knack,' was hooked.

Chapter Six

Midmorning on Thursday, April 25th 2013, six days before the refueling outage at Desert Canyons, was routine. Dax was enjoying a five-day work break between his last midnight shift and the start of his day shift rotation on the 27th. A radio played in the background, and Dax kicked back in a patio chair looking at a flyer for the big classic auto show next week at the convention center in Los Angeles. The small second-floor balcony was just big enough for one chair and overlooked a parking lot, some industrial buildings, and a little of the brown, manzanita scrub brush in the distance. The manzanita was heavier than normal from the heavier-than-normal rainfall over the winter. Fire season was going to be active. Dax didn't see the view, or the lack thereof. He was salivating at the prospect of the upcoming auto show. It was too bad that Dax started day shift on Friday with the rest of his crew, and would be on days until the auto show was over. Maybe he would attend an evening session if he could get away from work early enough.

Dax should have been reading the Floor Operator Training manuals stacked on the floor next to him, but he was feeling uncharacteristically lazy and couldn't muster any solid motivation. Dax had taken the written portion of the floor operator's qualification test two weeks ago but hadn't heard the results yet. If he passed the written (and he was sure he did), he could anticipate the oral board in the next few months. Two qualified Operations Shift Supervisors and the RADCON manager would get four hours to delve into Dax's knowledge of every floor level operating procedure in the plant. It was a formidable amount of information to know by heart and be able to discuss in finite detail. Dax was sure he was ready and understood the need for this level of expertise. The utility would be entrusting him with the operational safety of a two-billion-dollar nuclear power plant.

He still couldn't get motivated. He wanted to see the automotive works of art shown in the flyer. Yes, maybe he'd go one evening.

His cellphone rang, and Dax went inside to answer it. His phone was a simple, three-year-old Motorola Razor. It was old and basic as a sack of rocks. Dax accepted his phone's limitations with some resignation. He didn't get many calls, anyway. He'd thought about buying one of the new generation phones that recently hit the market. The phones were inexpensive. However, they came with an expensive per-call contract that he could not afford. But again, he didn't receive many calls, anyway.

"Dax, speak to me," Dax answered, expecting a glib retort.

"Good morning, Dax, this is Chief Operating Superintendent Thomas Brown. Have you got a few minutes?"

Dax stood up straighter out of respect, became more serious, and answered, "Yes, Mr. Brown. What can I do for you?"

Thomas picked up the pace of his words, "Dax, as you know, we have a refueling outage coming up in a few days. It's going to take a lot of extra operations coordination. I'm looking for a couple of people to go on an offset shift, and I would like you to be one of them. It'll mean a lot of hours and a lot of overtime. Instead of starting on day shift in two days with your regular crew, you will come in at 4 a.m. and get off at noon, seven days a week until a week after the outage is complete. That way, you can coordinate the last four hours of the midnight shift with the first four hours of the day shift and provide a smooth shift-change transition."

Thomas continued, "You'll have several assignments. I want you to be the operations representative observing the maintenance and refueling crews around the plant. They'll all be performing their own assignments with their own objectives in mind. I want you to observe their work and keep operational safety in mind. You'll be Plant Operations' eyes and ears out in the plant. I will also expect you to take a student or two in tow, when they are around, and do some teaching. You are a natural teacher, and the students like you."

"Thank you," was all Dax could squeak out.

Then, Thomas's voice took on a mockingly serious tone, "Of course, I'll expect you to spend a lot of time studying your ops manuals. It seems you've passed your written boards. You did well, top ten percent, congratulations. I've tentatively scheduled your oral boards for the first Wednesday after the end of the refueling outage. This outage will be a good opportunity for you to see some of these procedures in action. If you're lucky, you'll get a lot of study time in the quiet moments. You're going to have a very busy next few weeks."

"Thank you. Wow, I passed my written. I'll be there, 4 a.m. on Friday," Dax confirmed. "Have a great day, Mr. Thomas." Dax hung up. Oh no! Did he call his boss Mr. Thomas? His boss's name was Thomas Brown. How could they believe he could remember a complicated startup procedure when he couldn't remember his boss's name?

He took a second to reflect. *Wow*, Dax thought to himself, *I passed my written! Woohoo! I AM Good. I AM exceptionally good. Oh man, oh man, oh man! I passed my written.* Dax danced around the small deck as though he might create rain. Then, reality set in. Dax realized that this also meant his oral boards would be next! He thought, *my oral boards may be in as little as three or four weeks. I'm so far behind, so far behind. Oh man, oh man.*

Dax was reaching for the operations manual on top of the pile, when he realized that his afternoons would be free. He could go to the auto show. As soon as the work slowed down, he could take an entire afternoon, go to the auto show, and indulge himself. It also meant that he would be in the thick of performing all the pre-outage and shutdown procedures that he might need to know for his oral boards.

He made a quick sign of the cross and thanked The Lord that someone with his humble beginnings could work his way into such an important and prestigious job as operator of a nuclear power plant. Only in America would he find such opportunity.

Dax did have an almost tragic childhood. At 18 months old, he was sole survivor of a car accident involving him and his parents on the Greek island of Naxos. When no relatives came forward to claim him, he became a ward of the state. The bishop of the local See (church parish) for the Orthodox Catholic Church (Greek Orthodox Church) accepted responsibility for him as a ward of the local parish on Naxos. While the bishop had legal custody, all the members of the church adopted the boy as their own. Dax grew up with at least twenty mothers and a dozen fathers. He never lacked for someone to help him with his homework, someone to play soccer with, or counsel him on playground courtesy.

Dax didn't disappoint. He was bright, excelled in school, and finished high school at fifteen. He earned a degree in mechanical engineering from the University of Athens at nineteen. Dax's most endearing trait was his effusive personality. He was 'over-the-top' outgoing, kind to everyone, and liked by most. Early in life, he adopted a phrase that he let guide him: "Life is a game of skill, not of strength." He intended to live life with skill and daring. Dax was big and strong and could have been considerably more physically intimidating than he already was. He could have been a bully, but he wasn't. He didn't have the personality for it. It would have interfered with his enthusiasm for life. Dax's positivity was his biggest asset. It was certainly a contributing factor to his receiving a full scholarship to UCLA to study the effects of nuclear radiation on reactor materials. At twenty, he moved to Southern California, and two weeks later, he started classes at UCLA. Two weeks after that, he applied for a student internship at the local utility. The utility was building a nuclear power plant, and he thought it would be a great place to gain some experience in his chosen field. The utility hired him the day they received his application. They needed to fill twenty preapproved intern slots as soon as was practical.

So, there he was in Southern California. He had a full scholarship and a paid internship at the public utility that paid him enough to rent a small, one bedroom apartment overlooking a parking lot and some industrial buildings. He was surviving well, but he had a burning desire for one more thing.

Dax wanted to be a citizen of the United States and had started the application process. He was feeling displaced with no family, few friends, some language difficulty, and confusion with local customs. He was a displaced Greek citizen in the United States. Working half-time at the utility, spending every other available second studying for his classes, and preparing for his citizenship exams, however, left him with little time to be lonely. The utility helped by providing glowing reports for Dax and enthusiastically recommended that the government grant him citizenship.

Six months later, he walked into a courthouse to take his oath of citizenship. He knew it was a big day for him but didn't expect the impact that it would have on him. When Dax walked into the courthouse, he was a Greek immigrant who still had some difficulty with the language and customs. When he left the courthouse, he was an American citizen. He could vote. He could sit on a jury. He could own a gun. He was an American citizen with an excellent knowledge of the Greek culture and the Greek Islands. That day, he became an American who spoke excellent Greek.

Now he'd been out of school for two years, with his PhD in nuclear materials. He'd been an employee of the utility for four years and spent the last eight months as a training floor operator at Desert Canyons. He was not feeling displaced any more. He was part of a larger family. He had friends and security in his new life, and soon, he was going to be a floor operator in a nuclear power plant in California. In a few days, he would get to perform or, at least, witness all the procedures that he had been studying for months. He might even get to supervise some of them. Dax was worlds away from being an orphan in the Greek Isles, and he was on top of the world. Dax went back to his training manuals with a renewed gusto.

At that same moment when Dax was talking to Mr. Brown, Josef, who had now assumed the name Babar Collins, was sitting down at his home computer. He was waiting for the answer to a question he had posted on a dating bulletin board two days ago. Anyone could place a notice on a bulletin board and, depending on the privacy settings of the bulletin board, anyone else could review all the existing postings. As far as The Family knew, no American government agencies monitored the bulletin boards. No one was watching for terrorist communications among the lovelorn.

Josef's ad read, "Four-foot-ten-inch-tall male seeks contact with retired, female, French model. Previous relationship has run its course. Desperately seeking new relationship." He had posted a phony name and number in the ad. He didn't design the ad to bring a response. In fact, if he ever got a response, he would ignore it. The answer would come in the form of a new, unrelated ad. There was no continuous communication stream to follow.

The Family monitored selected bulletin boards and read every posting within twenty-four hours. Josef knew The Family had received his message. Josef would receive the answer and new instructions in the form of a new ad.

Josef would delete his listing in forty-eight hours and The Family would post their answer in the next day or two. Since Josef was expecting an answer, he also read all new ads on that bulletin board. As before, he did not answer the ad, so there was no communication trail to follow.

The answer he was expecting was in this morning's postings. It read, "Female, New York City police officer seeking same for relationship. My hobbies include taxidermy on gypsy moths from the Antarctic. My favorite event is the Lake Pontchartrain Hot Air Balloon Festival in July. I was born on December 15th, 1985, in LaPlace, Louisiana. Opening day is the best time to see the balloons."

The next meeting would be at the Hot Air Balloon Festival in LaPlace, Louisiana. The next major *event* would be in, or close to, LaPlace, Louisiana. He would arrange for some apartments, buy a car or two, and possibly a swamp boat. He would also scout the area and see if he could guess the industrial complex that might be the next target.

Josef turned off his laptop, unplugged the power and internet connections, and put the laptop in the trunk of his car next to the two boxes of personal effects that he'd packed earlier that morning. He didn't bother to return to the apartment. He had spent two days cleaning, sterilizing, wiping down surfaces, removing fingerprints, erasing all traces of Josef. He bleached the drains, vacuumed everything, then threw the vacuum cleaner into a different dumpster than the one he used for disposing of the vacuum bag. Before stepping away from the dumpster, he took a small pair of shears from his pocket and cut all his Josef Asseri identification into confetti. He threw the shears into the dumpster and put the confetti in his shirt pocket. He would drop a piece of ID confetti every few miles along the highway as he drove to LaPlace. He completed the transition by taking several identification documents for Babar Collins of Boston, Massachusetts, from his pocket. When he got to Louisiana, he would apply for a Louisiana driver's license in the name of Babar Collins. Babar, alias Josef, got into his car and started his long drive. Maybe he would take the southern route along the Mexican border.

Babar/Josef couldn't wait for May 1st. He was excited. Of course, he would have to watch the festivities on CNN.

Chapter Seven

On Friday, April 26th, five days before the start of the refueling outage, Brian Sing started his first day on the day shift rotation. He spent the morning reviewing the procedures and re-checking the checklists of the various groups that would be working that day. He was looking for operations safety concerns, fire safety concerns, personnel safety concerns, and whatever else he could find. It was a few minutes before 10 a.m. At noon, Lenell was coming to the control room to have lunch with Brian in the operations conference room at the back of the control room.

An alarm went off in the control room, and Brian turned to check it out. The control room operator stepped over to the console and announced, "Plant Air Compressor B Auto Start," in a clear, concise voice. Operators had configured Air Compressor B to 'top off' the compressed air tanks whenever the pressure got low. This automatic operation replaced the compressed air consumed by the plant operations. This was normal. The printer rattled to life as the computer made a duplicate entry.

Brian looked up, past the computer, past the control room operator to see Jack Smithson, the Desert Canyons Plant Manager (the single manager responsible for every aspect of Desert Canyons), standing a pace or two inside the back door. Jack nodded to Brian and gestured toward the conference room. Brian nodded back and followed him.

"Christina, you have the control room. I'll be in the conference room," said Brian. Christina Belvoir was Brian's control room operator.

"I have the control room, Brian," Christina echoed without looking up.

After he closed the conference room door, Jack turned to Brian and said, "Hi, Brian. I have two things. Judy and I are having a little dinner party at our house Tuesday evening before the outage, and we'd like you to come. 7 o'clock. Judy's making that Cajun Bisque you like so much." He grinned, knowing he had sealed the invitation.

"Oh, yeah, I'll be there. I wouldn't miss it. Can I bring anything?" Brian answered.

"It's casual, jeans and loafers, four couples. Bring a guest. And, uh, Judy asked that, if you have time, would you bring a platter of your Bayou Eggs?" Jack sat down in one of the comfortable conference room chairs and took on a more serious expression.

"Done," Brian said.

"The other request is a little more complicated. The NRC has been testing the waters with an idea to re-structure the format requirements of the nuclear power plant license renewal request. They've asked the larger utilities to appoint a representative to a peer review committee. The utility asked me, and I'm asking you," he paused.

"What does it entail?" Brian asked, raising his eyebrows. "It sounds like an interesting opportunity."

"Oh, it is. It would mean having your name on most of the new NRC documents relating to licensing renewal requirements. We both know that being a contributing author to NRC documents is a good thing."

"A career maker," Brian was already weighing the possibilities.

"The focus of the investigation is simple to put into words, but may not be simple to put into practice. In the past, the NRC required the maximum compliance for every subject area related to the licensing application for all nuclear power plants.

The NRC has decided that this may be unreasonable and expensive. Take two plants: Abrams, on the Mississippi River Flood Plain, and Desert Canyons. The area around Abrams floods, what, every three years with a major flood every seven? Here, it would take a major ice age to cause a flood, yet, both plants have the same licensing requirements for flood protection equipment and procedures," he explained.

"Under the new criteria, all plants would be required to first evaluate the extent of the flood threat for their plants, and second, present a plan that would protect their power plant from their level of flood threat. It might mean a fortune in savings on unnecessary equipment and procedures in exchange for a little effort in preparing our next license renewal. We don't yet know the impact that this new license protocol might mean for us."

Jack paused until Brian looked attentive again.

"That's where you come in. There's a teleconference scheduled at 10:00 a.m., D.C. time, next Wednesday morning. That's 7:00 a.m. here. We'll have it routed to the Pacific Crest Conference Room. I'd like you to participate, take notes, listen to the discussions, and provide a written analysis. I want your personal evaluation of what you think the benefit/cost ratio and pitfalls will be for us. When the time comes and this proposal is more developed, your recommendation will carry a lot of weight."

Brian thought for a minute, then said, "Seven a.m. on May 1st? Isn't that an hour before I'm supposed to start shutting down this reactor and isolating the plant for a refueling outage?"

"Yeah, I know. All I want is for you to log into the teleconference, listen, and ask a few questions. Be present. You can do a written report later. You'll be our man on this. Knowing the NRC, it'll be a long, slow process at best. But I want you to be involved."

"Okay. Where are you routing the call? Oh yeah, Pacific Crest Room. I will represent the utility at the NRC teleconference, thanks." Another alarm sounded in the control room. Brian looked around, distracted. "I must go. I'll take the call and let you know." He stepped back into the control room.

Brian wasn't interested in the alarm. Christina could handle it. Brian wanted to get out from in front of the plant manager so he could think about this for a minute. Being a contributor or a signer of any NRC Guidance document was a career changer. He would be a national nuclear licensing authority, and his value to the utility would go up proportionally. Yes, he would take this call and make himself invaluable. He even fantasized that it might lead to his being a consultant to the NRC or an NRC policy advisor. Now, he was looking forward to May 1st even more than before. As he walked around the control room trying to look involved, he was singing to himself, "Something tells me I'm in to something good…"

He thought about his lunch with Lenell Spector in a few minutes. This would give the two of them more to talk about.

As one might expect, not everyone on an operating shift at a nuclear power plant could take their mid-shift meal break at the same time. As often as not, shift workers were too busy to take a formal meal breaks at all. Brian's usual practice was to let the other members of his crew pick their meal times. Then, if the workload permitted, Brian would take a break. He had gotten used to eating at a small table in the back of the control room while he monitored the action in the control room. On slow days, Brian liked to buy lunch from the 'roach coach' that parked outside the security fence and eat at the picnic table next to the truck. This truck was old, rusty, and seemed to lack certain sanitary attention. The owner/operator wasn't very friendly, either. The food, on the other hand, was hot, spicy, tasty, and filling.

Today, however, things were different. Lenell had volunteered to get lunch at the roach coach and bring it to the control room. She said that she knew that Brian would be busy. He liked the idea of lunch with Lenell. He liked their lunches together and the opportunity to spend time with her.

Brian and Lenell had first met standing in line at the roach coach deli. Brian's favorite was 'Jose's Lunch Burrito' special with Mexican fries for eight dollars. Lenell also liked the Lunch Burrito, but without the fries. Both liked a bargain and, as fate would have it, both were punctual people to the degree of obsession. They ended up standing in line near each other almost every time

Brian went to the coach. It happened so often that Lenell began to suspect that Brian was doing it on purpose. It wasn't long before they struck up a casual conversation and began mee-ting in the line on purpose. On a couple of occasions, Brian had sug-gested that they sit at the picnic tables outside and have lunch together, but today, Lenell was bringing lunch to the control room. This was fortunate, because Brian wanted to ask Lenell to go to the boss's dinner and to tell her about the man he saw leaving the plant the other night.

At 11:45 sharp, Lenell step-ped into the back to the control room and waited for Brian to notice her. When he did, she pointed to her watch and mouthed, "Good time?" He gave her a thumbs-up and went back to work. Lenell walked down to the roach coach and bought their lunches. At 12 o'clock sharp, Lenell came back into the control room and went into the conference room with-out a word.

After a quick look around, Brian announced, "Christina, you have the control room."

Christina stepped back from her current task and surveyed the control room. "I have the control room, Brian," she answered.

Now Brian was free to enjoy lunch. He stepped into the conference room and took in the aroma of hot burritos.

"Hi," Lenell said brightly. "Hot, gourmet lunch from the roach coach is served. Sorry, no Mexi-Tots, today. I got BBQ chips instead."

"Chips are fine. You look like you're in a good mood. Having a good day?"

"Kinda, it's just a really busy, really good day. How's the prep work for the shutdown going?" She smiled back.

"Same as you, really busy, really good, and no surprises. I don't like surprises before a shutdown," he reflected and sat down. "I'll have to make this a short lunch, though. With everything going on, we need two people in the control room."

"No problem." She opened his bag of chips and handed him a burrito.

He took a small bite and said, "Jack came by a few minutes ago."

"Jack?" she inquired.

"Jack Smithson, the plant manager."

She nodded.

"Jack and his wife, Judy, are having a dinner party at their house on next Tuesday evening, 7:00 p.m., informal, 'jeans and loafers' he said. I was wondering if you would go with me, if you're not busy. I'll let you try one of my Bayou Eggs." He smiled the most ingratiating, boyish smile that he could muster and waited for her to accept his invitation before he continued. He added with a tone that implied that the answer was a foregone conclusion, "I know it's not much notice, but I'd like you to go with me." He paused again at her silence.

Lenell thought, *I knew he could do it, a dinner invitation and at our boss's house. It's about time.* Lenell had decided that if Brian had not asked her out on a formal date by the end of the refueling outage, she was going to invite him to dinner at her place.

"I would love to." She said with a pleased smile. "Uh, 7, do we bring anything? What's a Bayou Egg?"

"Write down your phone number and address. I'll pick you up at 6:55, sharp. A Bayou Egg is a creation of mine. I hard-boil and cool a dozen eggs. I shell them and then roll them in cayenne pepper. Then, I wrap them in a layer of sausage mixed with Indian spices, a home recipe. I deep-fry the whole thing in oil. Then, I slice them in half down the long axis as any surgeon would do (engineers) and open them. I serve them on a platter like a deviled egg. I recommend a dab of sour cream on top. There's no way that Bayou eggs are diet food, but they're addictive if you like having your sinuses ventilated. Call me if your plans change."

Her mind was somewhere else. *Tuesday night, casual, jeans and loafers? I'll need a new outfit! I'll need some new shoes, too.* Aloud, she said, "They sound delicious, like a solid heart attack bomb."

"Great! It's a date. It should be interesting. It'll have to be in early, though. Tuesday's going to be a major stress day for me," He smiled, pleased with himself. What he meant was, *I like you and I don't want to push you too fast.* He took another bite of his burrito, but didn't taste it.

"You also asked me to keep an eye out for anyone unusual going through plant doors while I was touring the plant?"

"Yes?" Lenell sat a little straighter and turned more toward Brian.

She forgot all thoughts of a new outfit or the dinner party. She knew that there was something not quite right about the rogue door open requests, and Brian might just have a significant piece of information for her. As he started to speak, she put a hand on his forearm as if to help him realize the importance of the event, as well.

"On my last night of midnight shift, I saw someone leave the plant that I don't think belonged there. A few minutes before midnight, someone I didn't recognize exited the plant through the Maintenance Building, parking lot exit. I didn't think about it until later, but he shouldn't have been using that door. Without a valid key card, opening that door at night will set off an alarm in the control," he explained.

"Really, what night was that?" she asked, forgetting her burrito.

"Sunday or Monday... it was the 22nd," he glanced at her hand on his arm. As much as he wanted it to mean something, he deduced that the hand was just a show of intense interest in the new discussion. Still, he made no move that might cause her to withdraw her hand.

This discussion was important to Lenell. Brian decided to make it an important subject for him as well. He tried to remember any other details that might be of interest to Lenell. Nothing came to mind.

Lenell continued, "I had several anomalies in the access report one night last week. There were several entry requests for people that couldn't have been in the plant and shouldn't have had access to the doors, all about midnight. It seemed to me that someone was wandering around the plant, randomly, in and out of several spaces."

"Randomly, huh?" he asked. "Do you remember which other doors? Do you still have the reports? I'd like to see them. I may have seen the event that triggered one of these bogus entries. At the least, I'll know what to look for when I'm on the plant floor"

She answered, "I don't remember which doors. I think the Turbine Building access door outside The Commons (the employee lunch and breakroom) was one of them. I have the reports in my desk. Something else, the reports show different incorrect people on different reports for the same entry request. Seems like when I call for a report, some of the names change. It's confusing. I can't explain how that would be possible. I've tried to talk to Richard about it, but he blows me off every time. In fact, he has not given me his full attention on any subject lately. I'm getting the impression that something is going on and I am on the outside looking in. I don't like being in the dark. Look, I have meetings all afternoon, but I'll pull the reports out and stop by when I can."

Then, she thought to herself, *Yeah, I have meetings this afternoon, at Devon's Boutique. I need to go shopping for a new casual outfit, and shopping for a new outfit trumps chasing a programming error.*

"Okay, I'll be interested to see names, doors, and times when you can."

"I do have another bit of news, for me, anyway," he said as he finished off his burrito.

Lenell popped a chip into her mouth and raised an eyebrow.

"It's another reason that I need to get in early Monday night. I'm scheduled for a 7:00 a.m. conference phone call with the NRC, Wednesday morning." He explained his new assignment and responsibilities to her. Lenell had been around long enough to understand the possibilities of the opportunity that management had bestowed on Brian.

They talked for a few more minutes about the NRC assignment, and then Brian said, "I'm sorry to have to break this up. Thanks for lunch, but I need to get back to work. This place doesn't run itself."

"No problem," Lenell said as she started to pick up the paper wrappers. "You go. I'll clean up."

"Thanks, again, for lunch," he said. Her presence had mesmerized him to the point that he began to forget his manners. "If I don't see you before, I'll see you Tuesday, 6:55. Don't forget the printouts." Then he was gone, back to his world, back to the control room.

Back in his world, a more formal Mr. Sing said, "Christina, I have the control room. Anything new to report?"

Christina looked up, "Nothing new. You have the control room." To herself, Christina thought, with a silent smile, *Yeah, control room nothing. You have a new girlfriend.*

As Lenell picked up the rest of the lunch debris and wiped the table, she looked out through the glass wall of the conference room at Brian. She liked what she saw: Tall, dark, handsome, and a commanding presence in every room that he entered. In a self-satisfied, singsong voice, she said, "and, he asked me to dinner."

Lenell had to hurry to make it to her 12:30 meeting on time.

She didn't look back as she left the control room, and neither did Brian.

Chapter Eight

All was quiet on Tuesday, the day before the shutdown. Brian and Christina ran the control room until 4 a.m. Dax worked until noon and then went to the car show. Mierie watched sitcoms and ate pizza all day. Alex James took the day off and fretted. Josef arrived in LaPlace and drove around a while, looking at the oil refineries that lined the banks of the Mississippi River.

Lenell was slammed all day with work. She reviewed and approved key copy requests, signed off on door access requests, and shuffled a mountain of paper. She had spent all weekend shopping and thinking about the dinner party. She still wasn't satisfied with the outfit she had chosen for the evening. The single decision that she had made, for sure, was that her shoes were not adequate.

At 4:30, Lenell closed her office and shut her computer down for the day. She was bailing on work uncommonly early so she could do some quick, last-minute shopping for *nicer* shoes. She still flushed a bit of romantic delight that Brian had finally asked her out. Thinking about Brian's good fortune with the NRC task force reminded her that last Friday, he had also mentioned seeing someone unusual exit the Maintenance Building at midnight- wrong time, wrong door.

She was miffed at herself for this uncharacteristically girlish excitement over her pending evening with Brian. It was too much of a distraction from her work. She shouldn't have let her excitement drive out the thoughts of the possible bogus door open event at the Maintenance Building exit, what, the 22nd, over a week ago now? She had her first solid lead and was too distracted to follow up on it. On the other hand, she was grateful that he had listened to her concern over the discrepancies in the door access log and had taken the time to notice the potential event. She still hadn't given him the printouts. It wasn't a priority for her, yet. She sat back down and pulled open the bottom desk drawer to get the printouts. The bottom drawer was empty. The printouts were gone!

After a moment of confusion, she turned to her computer thinking that she could do a quick research for the one event, but she had already shut the computer down for the night. She thought about calling Brian, but it was late, and she was sure he had left for the day. She also thought about calling her boss, Richard, but dismissed the idea. He had something else on his mind, something major. His indifference to her findings and his trivializing her concerns were frustrating. He was ignoring her, and she did not like it.

Then it dawned on her that Richard might have taken the printouts. Outside of Brian, Richard alone knew about them. Was Richard thinking that she might be altering the records? Was something illegal going on? If so, was she a suspect? After a moment, she let herself think a weak, unconvincing, 'nah.' She would see Brian tonight and ask his opinion again. He, of all people, knew the pulse of the plant. If all else failed, she might try to get the plant manager's ear. She wanted to see his reaction when she brought up the subject. She also resolved to request new printouts the first thing in the morning. She put her stapler upside down in the middle of her desk to remind her. She wouldn't forget again, and, as Scarlet O'Hara said in *Gone with the Wind*, "Tomorrow is another day." Right now, it was time to go home and get ready to go to dinner.

True to his word, Brian pulled into the parking lot of Lenell's condominium complex at 6:55. She met him at the door and invited him in.

"Can we be five minutes late?" she asked. "I have something I want to talk to you about."

"Sure. What's up?" he asked. "You look sensational, by the way." Brian didn't notice her new shoes.

"Thanks." *Typical nerd, he didn't notice my shoes,* she thought. Science nerds didn't naturally notice something as mundane as a woman's shoes.

"I told you that I would bring those printouts to you. Well, I've been so busy that I forgot until today. I was going to bring them tonight, but when I went to get them out of my desk, they were gone. I don't understand. Why would someone take them? I'm beginning to suspect that something is going on, and that I need to be more involved."

"That *is* strange. I haven't put a high priority on this computer glitch, either. But maybe there's more to this than we suspect," Brian said pensively. "Can you run the reports again in the morning? Let's say something to Jack tonight and see what he says."

Good answer, she thought. "Yes, let's. We should go," Lenell walked toward the door. Now, she couldn't wait to get to the party. It should be an enlightening conversation.

They were both quiet as they walked out to the car.

As they pulled out of the parking lot, Lenell gestured to the covered tray sitting between them. "Are those your famous Bayou Eggs? They smell enticing," Lenell said in an effort to be a little more playful.

"They are. Have a look. See what you think."

Lenell lifted the cover off the tray and saw two dozen Bayou Eggs. They did look a little like deviled eggs, except that the yokes were intact. Each egg had half of a yoke, surrounded by half an egg white, rolled in cayenne pepper, surrounded by spicy sausage. The aroma was exotic.

"I've never seen anything like them. They look delicious."

As Lenell put the cover back down, she smiled at Brian and asked in a flirty, conversational tone, "So, Brian Sing, who are you? Where did you come from? How did you get to be a nuclear power plant supervisor?"

Then with a little grin she added, "I want to know your every secret."

"Oh! Such big questions. Do you want the long answers or the short answers?" he asked with a twinkle.

"Well, we have a few minutes. I guess short answers will have to do, for now," she prompted.

"Okay. Well, my family originally came from India. We own a family construction materials business here in Southern California. I've wanted to work in nuclear power plants for as long as I can remember. I graduated from high school in 1992 and went to college in the Army ROTC program. I got a bachelor's and master's in nuclear engineering in 1996 and 1997 and accepted a commission as an Army officer 1998." He paused and tried to gauge her interest level.

"Go on," genuine interest was obvious in her face.

With a nod, he continued, "I spent two years working with nuclear weapons, but didn't care for it much. First chance I got, I transferred to the Army Nuclear Power program."

"I didn't know the Army had nuclear power plants," she observed. "I know the Navy has nuclear powered ships and submarines, but the military runs nuclear power plants?"

He nodded, "Yes, the Army has nuclear power plants. The military utilizes them in remote places where there is no reliable power grid or fuel supply, like Antarctica and the north slope of Alaska. I worked at power plants in Virginia, Alaska, and Panama. I loved Panama, especially the people. They were the friendliest, most outgoing people I have ever encountered. Not that I'm a world traveler, you understand, but the people that I met in Panama were so genuine."

He continued, "I left the Army in 2001 and went to work for the utility here in Southern California. In 2003, I transferred to Desert Canyons, and last year, I made Operations Shift Supervisor. I like soft jazz and quiet walks on the beach," he grinned at his attempt at humor. "I do like soft jazz. How about you? What's your short story?"

"Me? I grew up in El Paso County, Colorado, a couple of miles and a century from Colorado Springs. In the sixth grade, I won a statewide writing contest. When I was a sophomore in high school, I got mono and had to be homeschooled for the second half of the year. I fell behind in my classes. The missed school left me lost in math and science to such a degree that I was never able to recover. After I graduated high school, I went to Texas to go to a church college. In my junior year, I met a man, quit college, and got married. That didn't end well. I went home for a few months and then came here. I've been with the utility ever since. I like to swim for exercise and my favorite hobby is genealogy. I have charted over 3,000 direct ancestors. I love the stories that go with them," Lenell said, almost in one breath. "That's me, the short story."

"You were married? I'll bet there's more of a story there. Emphasis on '*were married,*' right? So, what happened?" he asked.

"That would be a long story. Maybe another time." Lenell was momentarily a little self-conscious. She was giving up too much information too soon. Few people knew the details of her marriage and divorce, and she wanted to keep it that way. She had given her total trust to a man, and he betrayed that trust. It wouldn't happen again.

"We're here," she said to change the subject.

Indeed, they were parked in front of their destination. It was time to go in, eat, and make nice.

Jack made sure that everyone knew everyone else and that everyone had something to drink. Conversation flowed, and they relaxed. At 7:30, everyone sat down and started on their salads, seafood bisque, and wine. More conversation followed.

At one point, Brian heard one of the wives say something about recently receiving a copy of her grandparents' marriage license in the mail.

"Marriage license, wow," Lenell tuned in. "They can be an interesting source of information. Did you learn anything new?"

"I did! The license had my great-grandmother's place of birth on the back, Wisconsin. I didn't know it before. It's opened a whole new direction for my searches." Everyone tuned in to their line of conversation.

Brian said, "Lenell and I were talking about genealogy on the way over. It seems that she has some interesting stories about some of her ancestors." He looked at Lenell.

Jack looked interested. "Really? I'd like to hear a couple of them.

"Me too," his wife echoed.

"Well, I guess I could tell you about Dragging Canoe. He was a Cherokee Indian Chief in colonial days. As a boy, he kept pestering the tribal chiefs to let him join the war parties against the white colonists. The chiefs told him that he was too small and too young to go to war. He couldn't join the men on the war parties until he could drag a loaded war canoe from the village to the river by himself. From then on, he dragged as loaded a war canoe as he could handle everywhere he went, and the name stuck. I have a copy of a pencil sketch of Dragging Canoe made by a local Army officer at the time. The officer described him as an *uncommonly fierce fellow*."

Everyone sat in silence looking at Lenell. When no one spoke, she continued, "I also have a great ancestor on my mother's side who was a Hungarian princess. She later married a prince in Scotland and became a beloved Scottish queen. After she died, Pope Pius I made her a saint. Her name was De Atheling. The interesting thing is what happened next. It was customary for the Catholic Church to re-inter the remains of all saints to the catacombs of the Vatican. That's what Pope Pius I ordered.

Two grave-diggers dug down to retrieve Saint De Atheling's remains, but they were unable to lift the coffin from the open grave. Two stronger men tried to lift the coffin and they failed. Next, as many men as would fit in the grave surrounded the coffin. They couldn't budge it. When Pope Pius I heard the story, he ordered that they restore the grave. If Saint De Atheling was that determined to stay in her beloved Scotland, then so be it. To this day, she is one of the few saints buried outside of Rome."

"That's fascinating. You have a famous saint in your direct ancestry?" someone asked.

"Actually, I've found seven saints in my direct ancestry," she added. "There were seven saints, various kings, and queens from England to Russia, sea captains, military men, plantation owners, and adventurers. Of course, there is also one great ancestor who ran a house of ill repute in Boston and a nine times great grandfather who was hanged as a horse thief."

"It must give you a deep sense of belonging to know so much about your ancestors," one of the other diners commented.

"It does," she acknowledged. "But the biggest thing that I've learned from all the stories is that all these people were so different from each other: different religions, politics, national loyalties, education, etc. But they were also the same in all the ways that matter. Except for a few people at the fringes, the super-rich, the hardened criminals, the fanatics; we're all just people. We'll all do anything for our families. We all love our children. We all want to make something of ourselves and leave a legacy. On the surface, we may all be different, but deep down inside, where it counts, we are all the same," Lenell stopped talking. She hadn't intended to dominate the conversation or to become so preachy. She looked around and noticed all eyes on her.

Jack spoke up, "I'll drink to that. Here's to being different and the same."

"Here, here." Everyone joined the toast.

Conversations broke back into smaller groups, and the dinner party continued. Lenell was surprised and more than a little pleased with herself. She looked at Brian and liked the smile of approval on his face. When he saw her notice him, he winked as well.

After dinner, Lenell found herself standing with Jack and one of the other wives while Brian stood at the dining room table telling the recipe for Bayou Eggs.

"Oh, I want to hear this," said Jack's wife and moved away.

Now Lenell was alone with Jack, so she took advantage of the situation. "Jack, I wonder if we could talk a little business for a second?"

"Yes," Jack said tentatively, "what's on your mind?"

In complete business mode, Lenell broached the subject, "I've been tracking some anomalies in the door access authorization system, lately. I tried to talk to Richard about it, but he's been avoiding me. I had some printouts in my desk that showed the problem, but they disappeared today. No one knew about them except Richard." She neglected to mention the fact that Brian also knew about the printouts. "Is something going on that I need to know about?" she looked at him and waited.

She didn't want to be the first person to speak after such a question. She knew that she would get more information if he spoke first. His face didn't betray guilt or collusion. He listened, smiled, and looked at his shoes for a second.

"Well, yes, something is going on," he said conspiratorially. "Don't worry about the printouts. Richard gave them to me. They are, uh, interesting. Yes, something is going on, and Richard is involved, not you. Legal has told me not to discuss it with anyone, and that, I'm sorry to say, includes you for right now. Look, when legal says that I can go public, you'll be one of the first people I call."

"Make sure that you're available at work for the next week or so. Also, you might want to update your resume. Trust me, I'm sure you're going to like the outcome of this situation," he smiled at her.

"Okay, I'll wait," she said. She thought, *My resume. I need another drink*. She wasn't sure she liked his political smile when he talked. It was a little too practiced. She now knew that there was a situation, Richard was involved, and Jack knew about it. Was Brian involved? Her hackles were up. She hated updating her resume almost as much as she hated being out of the loop. She never updated her resume unless she was looking for work. *Where's Brian? It's time to leave.*

She stepped over to where Brian was putting the cover on his empty food tray and asked, "Brian, can we call it an evening? I'm a little tired, and tomorrow is going to be a big day for both of us."

"Sure. Let's make the rounds and say good night," he answered.

Twenty minutes later, before Brian could even put the car in drive, the words started pouring out of Lenell. "I talked to Jack about the computer anomalies and the missing printouts. Brian, he knew about them." She related the conversation as she remembered it. She also told him about her apprehension. "Why do I need to update my resume? Why is this all so secretive? I'm a little concerned."

"Lennie, we're not firing you. You and I both know that you're doing a fantastic job, well above your assignment. I don't know what's going on, but I have a good ear at the plant. You're not in trouble. Besides, he said that you'd like it, whatever it is, right?"

"Brian, I, umm, uh, don't care for nicknames," she said, "But, you are right. I don't think that I've done anything wrong, either. I know I'm reacting to my past, a little. I blindly trusted a man once, and he hurt me. I won't let it happen, again." She lost herself in her thoughts.

After a minute, Brian said, "If I can change the subject, I'm curious about the long story surrounding your first marriage?"

With a small laugh, she said, "That was quite a fiasco," trying to buy time while she collected her thoughts. She didn't share the whole story often, so she didn't have a polished presentation.

She wanted to keep the story simple, with minimal emotions. "I attended college for three years at a Christian college north of Dallas, Texas. I met a local Deputy Sheriff named Tim Hayden and fell in love. I quit school and married him. His mom and dad were delightful people and made me feel like a part of the family, but he also had a brother and sister, and they made my life hell. A few years after we were married, I made a trip home to Colorado to see my parents."

Lenell paused, took a deep breath, and continued, "A few days after I got home, I got a registered letter containing divorce papers: no discussion and no explanation. I was blind-sided and I didn't like it. I felt so stupid." She stopped for another moment and then shrugged, "If I'm honest, 'no explanation' isn't the whole truth. I did suspect that he was having an affair with a woman that he worked with named Samantha. I asked him several times, but he always insisted that they were co-workers, nothing more. He was my husband. I trusted him. I believed him."

Brian lowered his voice and said, "You weren't kidding. There's no way to tell that tale in two sentences. What did you do? Did you ever get to talk to him again?"

"No. I never heard a word from him or any other member of his family. I did hear from someone he worked with that he married Samantha a few weeks after our divorce was final. I guess his affair with Samantha is no longer in question, is it?"

"I've heard / some stories in my time, but that may be the most cowardly thing I've ever heard. Have you ever tried to call him? Maybe, get some closure?"

"No, I know when I'm better off. I would still like some closure someday, some answers, you know. But the way I look at it, I'm lucky to be away from him. The whole situation could have ended a lot worse; I think. Do you want to hear the insult that went along with the injury? In the divorce papers, he sued me for his legal fees," she said with a forced, evil grin, then a quick, girlish smile.

Brian thought with more than a touch of sarcasm, *I should send this guy a thank you note. If he hadn't done what he did, I wouldn't have had the pleasure of her company this evening. I would never have known about Dragging Canoe. Yeah, I may have to send this guy a thank-you note. Tim Hayden from Dallas, Texas,* he thought to himself, *I'll have to remember that for later.*

They parked in front of her condominium. She was quiet. "It's been a wonderful evening, just what I needed. I had fun. Let's call it a night. I'd like to see you again." She looked at him in the dim interior, "As the outage winds down, why don't you come over for dinner some night? We can talk more." She did everything but flip her hair to act playful and flirtatious.

"Dinner would be great. See you at work tomorrow?"

He walked her to her door, kissed her goodnight, and went home. An hour later, they were both asleep.

Chapter Nine

As the dinner party broke up, Alex James prepared for the next morning. He worked in a daze, almost in a trance. He laid out his clothes: underwear, socks, boots, shirt, cargo pants, and the all-important cargo vest. He put his keys, a small amount of money, his passport, and his wallet in his pants pockets. Last, he clipped his 'Alex James' Desert Canyons ID to the outside front pocket of his vest, per regulations. His other four ID badges were in the front left pocket.

Bayani Bangit, a cultural exchange engineer from the Cotobato Power and Light Utility in the Philippines, provided ID-A. He was in the U.S. to study radiation control procedures and techniques. He would take his new skillset back to the Cotobato and become the resident RADCON expert in the Philippines. However, Bayani had a problem. The Cotobato Utility couldn't pay Bayani near enough to support the lifestyle he thought he deserved, and Bayani was going into debt. His family was in trouble. He needed a break. Six weeks before his scheduled return to the Philippines, a break by the name of Mierie (just Mierie) presented itself.

Mierie was willing to pay an exorbitant amount of money (a year's pay back home) for Bayani's ID. Bayani was going home. He didn't need the badge; after he processed out, it would be useless. It wouldn't access the computer systems or open any doors, and after he went home, the badge would be inactive. In short, Mierie couldn't do anything with this ID if Bayani waited until the day he left to give the badge to Mierie. True, the computer tracking system would keep a permanent record of the ID number, but the badge itself would be useless.

He would get a lot of money for nothing. So, a couple of weeks before he was due to leave, Bayani would "lose" his badge and get a new one, maybe even a temporary one. He decided to hold the contraband badge until the day he left, just to make sure. Bayani congratulated himself for his good fortune. Mierie congratulated Bayani on his wisdom.

Mierie obtained the second credential by sheer chance. As Bayani was processing out of Desert Canyon, he had to turn in his ID badge and sign a non-disclosure agreement. He had his ID badge clipped to the inside of his manila file. The processing clerk added it to a stack on the corner of the desk. The processing clerk entered some data into her computer and pressed print. Then, she went to get the receipt from the printer in the next room. On impulse, Bayani reached over to the pile of folders, took the top three off the pile, and set them aside. He opened the fourth folder, removed the ID badge, and put it in his shirt pocket. He closed the folder, restored the stack of files, and stared blankly at the Security First poster on the wall behind the desk. The whole thing took about four seconds.

Bayani finished out-processing without incident, and a security guard escorted him out of the building. His assignment was over. Later that evening, when he gave his "lost" badge to Mierie, he also gave him the stolen one.

Bayani said in a matter-of-fact tone, "I thought that if one badge was useful, two might be more so."

Mierie took the badge and was impressed how Bayani gave him the badge with no apparent reservations. Bayani didn't mention money, offered no strained negotiation, and no coercion. Bayani had shown respect and trust that Mierie would do right by him. Mierie liked that. He used the same matter-of-fact voice, "Very astute. Of course, I appreciate the second badge. I will wire you the money this evening."

Mierie smiled and put his hand on Bayani's shoulder. They were comrades, friends. Even with Bayani in the Philippines, it was best to keep him happy and comfortable with his part of the conspiracy. He looked at the second badge. It was for a Sharron Nelson.

The third and fourth badges were easier to obtain. Mierie lifted the third off a sweatshirt at a health club. He lifted the fourth off a jacket at a local bar while the owner visited the men's room. Both employees reported the losses to the security front office. Of course, the man reported his badge as lost at work, not lost at a bar. Both owners obtained new IDs with new numbers, but the security program kept both the new and the old numbers on file as a permanent, traceable record. The new file referenced the old file and vice versa. Both owners had an expired, inactive number in the computer.

Now Alex James had the four needed ID/key badges.

Alex James also put half of a three-by-five card in the same pocket.

He knew that Josef had a hard rule against writing anything down, but he didn't trust his memory. In stressful situations, his memory tended to fog up a little. It might be difficult to remember the phone number for the trigger box at the critical moment. He had written the phone number on the card. He had created a piece of paper trail. Alex was sure that no one would ever know because he also put a book of matches in the same pocket to burn the card over an open toilet and flush the ash. He knew he was smart enough to take this chance.

After he had prepared his clothes and breakfast to his satisfaction, he spread his prayer rug on the floor, facing Mecca. He prayed, meditated, and cleansed his mind. He would bathe and dress according to the dictates of his religion in the morning. For now, he prayed and relaxed. He let his mind drift as it wanted, and he remembered.

He remembered February 26th, 1993. He was twelve. His mother, father, uncle, older brother, and younger brother had come into the city for the day. They had driven themselves to town in his parents' red car instead of taking the commuter train. Suhad was attending a women's rights conference in the Regency Hotel. As one of the most respected members of the local women's movement, Suhad was a guest speaker. His father came along for a show of support. His uncle came along to entertain the boys, to take them on an outing on the city.

Adawi, his uncle, and brothers stood on the sidewalk across from the hotel, eating shaved ice treats they bought from a street vendor. His was vanilla. A coffee shop shared the building with the hotel where they would meet his parents. His older brother was a few steps down the sidewalk, apart, aloof. When they finished the icy treats, they would cross the street to meet his parents. As other participants came out of the hotel, Adawi remembered looking up into the sky and seeing a bird flying high above, seeming to stand still against the deep blue, morning sky. He remembered a gust of hot, dry summer breeze against his face like a wave of heat from an open oven door. It felt good in contrast to the shaved ice melting in his mouth. In that moment, his world was a silent photograph that he would remember forever.

His gaze traced down to the front of the coffee shop, and he remembered seeing every stone of the front of the hotel and coffee shop simultaneously disassociate from every other stone on the fronts of the buildings. The glass front became glitter. He saw each glass shard silently expand away from every other shard like a slow-motion dance of flying diamonds. He wondered at the silent expansion of the angry rust-brown dust boiling behind the diamonds. He remembered feeling his little brother slam back against him, and then himself slam back against his uncle. His shaved ice hit his chest and face. He remembered the confetti that was the buildings peppering his face and arms, leaving dirty little marks and spots of blood. Then, all was dark and silent as the concussion reached him. He hurt all over and he couldn't move. He passed out. When he came to for a moment, he heard angry men shouting somewhere nearby, then he passed out again.

Adawi's family never knew for sure, who had set off the bomb at the Regency Hotel and coffee shop, or why. It might have been the Muslim Brotherhood, rising to power in the area in 1972, trying to destabilize the government and gain control of oil fields. It might have been one of the oil companies trying to secure the profits from selling oil to the Soviets, or a drug cartel trying to eliminate a rival. It might have been a local warlord with a grudge against a guest at the hotel, or a group motivated by religious or political differences. It might have been the French, the British, or the Americans. The American CIA had been increasing its activity in the Middle East. It might have been simple, homegrown terrorism. There were so many possibilities in the Middle East at the time. One thing was certain: The women's rights conference in the second-floor conference room wasn't the target, and the innocent civilians at the coffee shop next door were tragically in the wrong place at the wrong time.

The next time Adawi woke up, he didn't hurt any more. In fact, he didn't feel much at all, only the comforting squeeze of a warm, soft blanket all around him. He was so relaxed that he wanted to keep his eyes closed and enjoy the pleasant feeling of floating. He wanted to smile at, well, everything. He knew he was in a bed; he could feel the sheets. The air was cool against his face, so he was indoors. He heard people mumbling nearby. There was no stress in their voices. He opened his eyes. His uncle and a nurse stood nearby, huddled in conversation. He had never been in a hospital before, so it took him a few anxious minutes to figure out that his uncle was talking to a doctor.

"Ummi….Abbun (mommy…daddy)?" he asked weakly. His uncle stepped quickly to his side and laid a hand on Adawi's chest.

"Everything will be all right, Adawi. Sleep, now. Rest," he said. Adawi did sleep, and he recovered. He recovered quickly.

Adawi's older brother died within minutes of the explosion from severe lacerations caused by broken glass. His younger brother died a few hours later from blunt force trauma after intercepting the stones that would have killed Adawi. Adawi and his uncle escaped unscathed save a few minor cuts and a temporary hearing loss. For Adawi, the tragedy was that his parents were also dead. The doctors never positively identified either Suhad's or Talib's remains. Adawi was the sole survivor of his immediate family. Fourteen other people died and seventy-one more were wounded in the attack on the coffee shop.

His aunt and uncle were the sole remaining adult family members that he recognized. They agreed to take him in and provide for him. And provide for him they did, after a fashion. His uncle worked all the time on his own small farm plots, and now, on Adawi's newly-inherited rose bushes. He had no time for his own children much less the son of a brother. Adawi's aunt resented this intruder and favored her own children with love, attention, and understanding. She also used the money from Adawi's roses to lavish gifts and luxuries on her children and pointedly neglected Adawi.

Adawi was already physically isolated because he couldn't keep up with any aerobic activity. Stress and anger caused his thinking to spin. He was small, weak, and a social outcast. Now he was without the support of the main adults that he had trusted his entire life. To his credit, he was also highly intelligent and reasonably self-assured.

It was this natural intelligence that caused the men of his uncle's mosque to notice him. They took him under their wing and taught him the

Koran. They taught him how to think critically on religious subjects, but also to listen to their particular interpretation. They talked of life's mysteries and argued religious philosophy with him. They liked his unique interpretation of scripture. They treated him as an equal and made him feel secure. They also listened to him, comforted him, and cried with him. They became his 'family,' his brothers, his mentors. He found acceptance and was part of an admired brotherhood. He liked his new brothers and he thrived under their influence.

One Imam named Khatib took a special interest in Adawi. Adawi admired the Imam's dedication to a simple life of limited luxury. Adawi also admired the Imam's knowledge and understanding of the Koran. Except for time spent in religious discussion, Khatib kept his distance from the other men. He always seemed to be meditating. He was strong and quiet. Adawi felt as though he would follow the Imam anywhere. The Imam was also Iranian, not Egyptian, and he had his own reasons for being in Egypt, his own agenda.

Khatib had an eye for talent and knew that Adawi had the kind of intellect for which he was searching.

The boy showed a skill with computers, and the Imam was sure that computer skills would have future value to The Family. The boy also had no family to speak of, and an internal bitterness that they could exploit. Even though the Imam had no knowledge of who was responsible for the bombing, he told the boy that it was the American CIA working for huge American oil companies who placed the bomb that killed his parents. According to the Imam's story, the target was an Egyptian oil company executive who had a negative opinion of doing too much business with the Americans. People were blaming the American CIA for every negative event in Egyptian daily life (justified or not), and, with no opposition to counter the message, the Imam was able to exploit and reinforce the boy's growing hatred for anything American. Khatib made sure that the boy received the 'proper' political education, as well as a complete computer engineering education. The Family would find a useful place for this boy. In a left-handed way, Adawi was lucky. The Imam also kept an eye out for people with other talents. He cultivated the gullible to be suicide bombers and the fearless to be soldiers. Adawi was lucky he was so smart and too weak to be either.

Adawi learned to use computers, to hack them, and make them do things that others could not. He learned word processing, spreadsheets, and computer-aided designing. He could make impressive 3-D renderings of complicated machine parts. He learned to use computer-based scheduling programs, publishing programs, and engineering programs. He learned as much about computers as possible, all in the name of Allah. He also learned to hate Westerners, particularly Americans. The Family found a special place for his anger.

For the next ten years, The Family educated and radicalized Adawi. He learned and practiced all the mantras, but he never excelled. He knew that he wasn't a born freedom fighter. He knew that he didn't measure up, so he drifted.

On a stunning fall afternoon in 2001, the Imam cancelled all classes and training. Teachers turned on televisions as everyone assembled in the biggest classroom. It was a little before two on September 11th; a news report showed one of the World Trade Center buildings in New York on fire. A senior camp training cadre commander shouted the details of the glory for one of the terror cells that had flown a plane into the side of the building. It was a spectacular blow against The West. This was their end goal.

As Adawi watched, the people around him rejoiced. They fired guns into the air, and shouted prayers and political slogans to the sky. Everyone danced in jubilation. Then, another plane hit the second tower. Adawi stared transfixed.

The others in the room exalted the brave martyrs who carried out the attack as heroes. They earned a guaranteed place in heaven by Allah's side. Their compatriots would tell stories and sing songs about these heroes for years.

Adawi looked at the celebration around him. Those martyrs were the role models Adawi wanted to emulate. He sat in silence and watched the twin towers burn. He would go to America someday. He would strike an equally-spectacular blow against the U.S.A. People would sing his name. He would earn his place at the right hand of Allah. He would belong.

As the first tower fell, all unnecessary parts of Adawi's previous life fell away with it. He didn't need anything in his life that didn't help him fulfill his destiny. He would be the most honored martyr of all time. That afternoon, The Son of the Lion died, and Alex James was born. He was twenty-one years old.

At a little past midnight on May 1st, Adawi, the boy, and his alter ego, Alex, the man, finally found enough peace to fall asleep.

Chapter Ten

At 3:30 a.m., Dax's alarm clock went off. With Dax's adrenaline level so high from both the car show last night and the prospects for work today, the alarm didn't get a chance to buzz twice. Dax wasn't merely excited; he was amped. If someone had viewed from the outside, it would have appeared that Dax went from reclining with his body flat on the bed, to standing straight up in one motion. He took four quick steps to the bathroom and started his morning shower routine. On the way out of the apartment door, he grabbed his breakfast from the fridge, a pita bread sandwich made from leftovers.

On the drive to the plant, he remembered the restored, yellow '61 Corvette Stingray that he had seen the afternoon before. He thought that he might just have to buy that beauty, or one like it, when he became a control room operator. A few minutes before 4:00 a.m., he parked in the employee parking lot and started his walking inspection. At 4:00, he walked into the control room.

"Good morning, Dax," said Downing. "How are you this morning?" Without pausing for an answer, he said, "When you get settled, please, go down and help Shawn with the Demineralized Water Still. When the Demineralized Water Storage Tank is full and the chemistries are complete, he's going to put the still into hot standby. When you're done, come back to the control room."

"On my way," Dax answered.

*****

As Dax left the control room, Alex James was floating a few inches above the ground. His withered arms and legs hung down in atrophy. The sky and earth were odd, the colors bizarre. He couldn't feel the air around him and he couldn't hear a sound. Everything was flat, like a photo. Rows and rows of two-inch-tall seedlings covered the landscape as far as he could see: peas, corn, cabbage, and lettuce. The seedlings were green, hardy, and basking in the life-giving sunlight. Alex saw Mohamed and Allah standing in serene silence, side-by-side on the horizon to the east. They smiled down at his accomplishments in his garden, but the all-powerful sun was getting too hot, giving too much light. He tried to block the sun, to cool the air, and to give the roots more water, but the seedlings started to wilt. He couldn't breathe. He looked to the east.

"Mohamed, help me." WAAHHH! Mohamed and Allah gazed on the scene with peace radiating from their auras. Neither seemed too disturbed that his field of seedlings was dying.

WAKHHH! Alex noticed that there were now hundreds of people standing next to Mohamed and Allah, in a big circle all around the horizon. WAKHHH! "Help me save the future generations of our garden." Alex couldn't breathe. "Help me, Allah. The sun is killing our farm." WAKEHH! WAKEHH! Alex was on the ground, now, on his hands and knees. He was trying in vain to save the seedlings. He saw small pools of water forming in the low spots around him. The water looked so cool and inviting. The pools were getting larger and deeper, but the seedlings were dying.

WAKEHP! Some of the pools join with other pools, as the water got deeper and deeper. The water was coming from out of the ground. WAKEHP! The dark water of the pools reached his knees and hands. It was refreshing. The feel of it on his hands was comforting. He felt like the dark water was inviting him to lose himself in its depths.

WAKE HP! The rows of seedlings were dead and gone forever. The water was everywhere, as far as he could see. It was up to his chest and so biting cold that it hurt. WAKEHP! His cares washed away. He was calm as he slipped below the surface. He looked up and saw it less than an inch away.

WAKE UP! He wanted to stay below the water, gazing up at the surface, but duty and glory called. He couldn't stay. The alarm clock woke Alex from his nightmare with a final blatant blast of sound. He couldn't breathe.

Calm down. Calm down. He cooed to himself in a soothing voice, *Calm down. Breathe, breathe, breathe.* He had been through this before. The insistent blaring of the alarm clock helped him to focus. "Calm down, calm down, breathe," he whispered aloud. His breathing and pulse slowed. When he could move his arms, he reached over and silenced the clock. Calmness returned to Alex James. He took one last deep breath. It was 4:00 a.m. The most significant day of his life had begun.

*****

At a little past four, Manuel Rojas was already awake. He was unable to sleep soundly. He rolled onto his side, turned off his alarm clock, and began his morning routine in silence. All he could think about was his overseas bank account and the lavish life that the money was going make possible.

*****

At 4:48 a.m., per the script, Alex James left his apartment for the seventeen-minute trip to the Desert Canyons security gate.

*****

At five minutes to five, Manuel Rojas left his silent house for the office.

*****

As Manuel drove down the quiet suburban street, Brian Sing's alarm went off. He wanted to have an hour or so to walk around the plant before his NRC teleconference.

*****

At 5:05 a.m., Alex James walked through the plant security gate, right on schedule.

*****

At the utilities' downtown office, the eager beaver morning crew trickled in to continue work on the outage. Manuel Rojas was among them.

*****

Lenell Spector's alarm went off at 5:30 a.m. As a rule, she didn't like getting up an hour early, but today was different. She was looking forward to an exciting day and wanted to get to work by seven. That way, she could reprint the missing computer reports and check some of the newer reports for new anomalies while Brian was on his teleconference call. She planned to meet him in the hall outside the control room for a minute and give him the printouts. She also needed to give him a one-minute tutorial on how to read them. If Lenell was honest with herself, she wanted to see him again, to talk to him again. She was more critical than normal picking her clothes for the day. While removing her blouse from its hanger, she noticed that her nails needed some attention. She believed that her flightiness was because she had new supporting evidence about her unauthorized door open investigation. She wanted this day to start. She wanted it to be eight o'clock.

*****

At ten minutes to six, Brian Sing arrived at the Desert Canyons employee parking lot. He had an hour to walk around and relax before the phone call, and two hours before he needed to relieve Downing. He wanted to avoid the control room for a bit longer, so he decided to go by The Commons, and see if anyone had brought in some pre-breakfast dough-nuts to eat while he walked around the plant.

Chapter Eleven

At 6:00 a.m., things started happening quickly. Mierie's bedside alarm clock went off, and he began to prepare for his day. His attention was laser focused on the script. He went over it again and again in his mind. To Mierie, nothing else was happening today, nothing else was important.

*****

Also at six, Dax entered the control room. The Demineralized Water Still was in hot standby. The other operators had left to make their hourly rounds and take log readings.

"The Demineralized Water Still is in hot standby. What's next, Chief?" Dax announced to Downing.

Downing turned, looked at him, and thought for a moment. Then he said, "Okay, Dax, go down to the student temporary office and see if there are any eager beavers in early. Take a couple of them down to the River Water Pump House. The computer says that there's some low-level liquid waste in the holding tank. Show the students how to set up the dilution/discharge operation. Explain the NRC release criteria. There's not much in the tank, so wait for it to finish. Explain as many of the other systems and procedures to the students as you can. We strive to teach."

Not the most glamorous job, Dax thought, *but I'll take it.* He left the control room with a smile on his face.

*****

As Dax was receiving his instructions, Brian was entering The Commons to get his coffee. There was one other person in The Commons, a man in a cargo vest and pants standing off to one side, watching the CNN feed on the overhead monitor.

*****

Alex had entered The Commons a few minutes before and retrieved his key. He had to wait until 6:04, anyway, so he watched the news. Unfortunately for Alex, the segment was on fashion and glamor. The repost angered Alex. Half-naked women paraded up and down a fashion runway. Their faces heavily painted to exaggerate pure sexuality and to tempt men into sin. His disgust was overwhelming. Anger burned his sensibilities. The newscaster was praising these women and the industry that supported them as a 'way-of-life' that all women should pursue. These were the people who tempted good Muslim men and women from the true path. As if he was trying not to throw punches, he clenched his fists and pursed his lips until they were thin, white threads. He felt the pulse of his anger begin in his ears but didn't try to calm his blood pressure. Alex enjoyed venting the moment of self-righteous indignation. He needed the release.

These are the devils responsible for my mother's death, he thought. They tempted her with their false gods, their painted beauty, and their promiscuous sex. If it hadn't been for people like these and their decadent culture, his mother might have stayed home where she belonged. She wouldn't have been trying to achieve a self-serving fame in their world. She wouldn't have been at the Regency Hotel or the coffee shop that day. She wouldn't have died in an explosion. He hated them. Rage rolled in him and contorted his face. He would make them pay.

Brian walked into The Commons at that exact moment. Brian barely noticed the emotional turmoil on Alex's face. He had often felt real anger at some newscasts. Brian found it insulting to his intelligence when the government and/or newscasters omitted some crucial component of a story that would have explained the sensational headline. On many occasions, Brian had wondered what the other half of the story was. It was as if they thought the average John Q. American couldn't cope with or understand the complete truth. It made him feel as though they, the news media, felt they were superior, and that the public was inferior. Even more aggravating was the fact that they seemed to think that all Americans were too sensitive to deal with the facts (or outright lies) that would not destroy the average American's sense of security. No, it wasn't Alex's obvious anger that caught Brian's attention. It was what happened next.

As Brian took his first sip of coffee, he commented, "The news can be aggravating, sometimes, can't it?"

Alex's demeanor flash-changed to one of calmness and serenity. An overly-indulgent smile replaced the angry grimace, and he relaxed his body. He was still sweating as he tried to cover his involuntary nervousness. Brian had expected this man to answer with some kind of agreement or confirmation. Instead, Brian saw a quick and practiced cover-up. The transformation was unnatural, downright disturbing. It seemed forced, almost practiced. He was suddenly too nice and too happy. This man was hiding something. Brian's hackles went up.

"Just watching the news," Alex said with an egregious smile and a gentle wave of the hand. "The pop fashion industry, what a crock." Alex, still shaking inside, turned to leave The Commons. Brian watched him go, wondering what that was all about. It was 6:04 a.m.

*****

A minute or two later, Dax entered the students' office and found a single eager beaver there, a college junior named Donny. If Dax remembered correctly, Donny was a premed student from Bakersfield, California. Dax remembered because Donny had shown everyone a picture of himself at a student orientation meeting at the medical school at Washington State University. Donny wore medical whites and was holding a human brain in his hand.

Dax said, "Good morning, Donny. You're here early. This is your lucky day. If you're free for the next couple of hours, I have some work to do at the River Water Pump House and you're going to help me."

Anything's better than sitting here all morning Donny thought and then said, "I'm game." Donny had to admit that this nuclear power plant stuff was pretty cool. Maybe he would investigate nuclear medicine as a specialty.

*****

Brian watched the news in The Commons for a few more minutes. There weren't any doughnuts.

*****

At 6:12, Manuel changed the ID numbers for the four stolen identities. He also changed the personnel ID number for Thomas Brown that would grant Alex the authority to enter the turbine deck. He made the last change as Alex turned to leave The Commons.

*****

As Brian stepped into the hallway, he had a small flash of realization. That man in the cargo vest had a temporary badge on, yet he turned right when he left The Commons. There were only private offices and the access door to the turbine deck to the right. A temporary ID shouldn't open any of the doors in that hallway. Brian was going to walk through the plant, anyway, so he decided to start with the turbine deck. Who was Mr. Cargo Vest and where was he going?

Brian walked the few steps to a turn in the hallway and looked around the corner. Mr. Cargo Vest was… gone. It was 6:16. Out of habit, Brian reached for the comms to call security, but he wasn't on shift yet, so he didn't have the phone. He started walking down the hallway. What was Mr. Cargo Vest doing?

*****

Brian entered the Turbine Building as Manuel Rojas restored Thomas Brown's assigned personnel ID number. Manuel didn't notice that Brian Sing had followed Alex into the Turbine Building.

*****

Brian didn't feel threatened or alarmed. Mr. Cargo Vest was in the wrong place at the wrong time, but he wasn't menacing. Therefore, Brian did little more than half-look for Mr. Cargo Vest as he continued his walk through the plant, checking everything that was going on around him. As Brian stepped onto the main turbine deck, he quickly scanned the voluminous space. No one was visible. He looked to the near stairwell on his left and then to the far stairwell at the other end of the turbine deck. Again, he didn't see anybody. It was too early to go to the conference room for the NRC call, so he decided to walk down the side of the main turbine generator to the high bay pit at the far end of the building. He checked bearing temperatures, oil sight glass levels, and others as he went. The temperature was right. The air smelled of oil and heat. Everything hummed normally. The familiar vibrations were reassuring.

When Brian reached the high bay pit, he looked over the edge and scanned the floors below. Mr. Cargo Vest was two floors below him, standing at an equipment storage rack. He was taking a piece of equipment down from the rack. Brian stood still and remained silent. He wanted to see what Mr. Cargo Vest was doing. Mr. Cargo Vest removed the protective plastic dust cover from a small pre-fabbed electronic box and shoved the covering back onto the shelf.

Brian looked back up to his floor level. At the far corner of the high bay pit was the door to the stairwell. Brian decided to go around the pit, down the stairwell, and come out of a stairwell door next to Mr. Cargo Vest.

Brian knew that he had to be quiet. He'd seen enough TV cop shows to know that if he shouted, "Hey you! Stop!" from two decks away, the suspect was going to run– *Duh*. What did the TV cops think a guilty TV criminal was going to do, stand there and wait for two police-men to walk up to him and arrest him? Brian moved with as much stealth as he could manage. He wan-ted to confront Mr. Cargo Vest and ask him what he was doing, not chase him all over the plant.

As Brian walked along the edge of the high bay pit, he focused his attention for a few seconds on the gauges on the Compressed Air Mani-fold mounted on the far wall. He al-ways checked these gauges when he passed this spot. Habits were hard to break. As he passed the corner of the pit, out of sight of Mr. Cargo Vest, he a had flash of understanding. Mr. Cargo Vest might be stealing the sto-red, excess equipment from the sto-rage shelves in the high bay. If this were the same man that he'd seen a few nights ago, it would explain why he was leaving the Maintenance Buil-ding complex via such a little used door, a door that opened into the par-king lot. Brian seemed to remember that the other night the man had some paperwork in his hands. He didn't remember if Mr. Cargo Vest was carrying any hardware, but then, he hadn't been looking for hardware. Brian went on higher alert, and his sense of urgency went up a notch or two. He might be confronting a common thief. He increased his pace as he reached the door to the stairs.

*****

At the same instant Brian turned away from watching Mr. Cargo Vest, Alex James looked up and saw movement two floors above him. He jolted as he recognized Brian Sing, one of the people he was supposed to avoid at all costs during this operation. Alex watched Brian as he walked along the guardrail. Brian never looked his way. Maybe Brian hadn't noticed him. Alex stood frozen until Sing was out of sight, then, even though he still had ten minutes until he needed to be at door PSB-34 (6:35 sharp), he started moving as quickly as possible toward the stairwell. He had to drop down one floor and go a hundred feet to the left to reach the maze of pipes outside the door to the Penetration Access Hallway. Alex needed to get lost in the maze of pipes for a few minutes. He didn't want to be out in the open if Sing came his way.

From then on, the movements of the two men looked almost choreographed as they walked through the plant. Alex rushed to the stairs and ran down to the ground floor as Brian came down the stairs above him. Brian saw movement in the stairwell's ground floor doorway and heard the ground floor door close. Mr. Cargo Vest was moving fast now, and Brian was surer than ever that Mr. Cargo Vest had something to hide. Brian dropped down the remaining flights of stairs as quickly as his feet would move, but he couldn't quite bring himself to run. Running was against safety rules, and people who ran had accidents. Accidents caused paperwork. The paperwork from needless accidents caused management to get upset. A perfect safety record was a major management goal and a perfect or near-perfect safety record and low year-end safety expenses showed well on a managers' year-end reviews.

*****

As Alex and Brian descended the stairs, Dax and Donny entered the River Water Pump House. Dax looked at the Liquid Waste Holding Tank level gauge. The tank was one third full. He estimated that it would take about two hours to complete a legal 'dilute waste' discharge. Dax thought, *Okay, Donny, time to learn.*

*****

Alex turned the corner into the piping alcove surrounding the door to the Penetration Access Hallway at the same instant Brian came out of the stairwell. Alex nestled into the maze of pipes and tried to blend in. He was sweating and breathing hard. He feared that his heart was making more noise than a herd of wild horses. It was good that the power plant made more noise than ten herds of wild horses. Still, he was sure that if Brian passed close enough, Brian would discover him. Alex didn't know what he would do if Brian saw him. The script didn't call for this scenario. Maybe he would jump out and overcome Brian with a surprise attack. He might kill Sing as a bonus, in the name of Allah. He liked that idea. It calmed him.

*****

Brian walked out onto the Turbine Building ground floor, no Mr. Cargo Vest. Across from Brian was a blank wall. To his right were the high bay roll-up truck door and the maintenance wing personnel door.

To his left was the access door to the Penetration Access Hallway and some small equipment rooms. Brian turned left, toward the Penetration Access Hallway. He didn't think that Mr. Cargo Vest went that way. The high bay was a dead end, and Brian was standing in the only exit. Mr. Cargo Vest would have trapped himself if he went to the left– not likely. Brian took three steps then remembered his encounter with Mr. Cargo Vest last week. He had been coming out of the Maintenance Building emergency exit near the parking lot. If Mr. Cargo Vest were stealing from the plant, he'd want to take his prize to his car. That made sense.

Brian stopped in his tracks, stood still, looked straight ahead, and listened for a moment. If he had looked to the left, he would have looked into Alex James's eyes. Brian thought, *If Mr. Cargo Vest is headed for the Maintenance Building emergency exit, I can still catch him.* Brian spun hard on his heels and headed for the access door to the Maintenance Building. He spun so fast that he did not see Mr. Cargo Vest standing among the pipes less than fifteen feet away.

In seconds, Brian walked through the Maintenance Building door and was gone. Alex looked at his watch. It was 6:32. He had three minutes to calm down and clear his head.

*****

At 6:33, Manuel changed Minerva Hopkins's personnel ID number to match ID-B. All was quiet at the home office. The dumb bastards were clueless.

*****

At 6:35, Mierie left his apartment. He wore a pair of old jeans, a flannel shirt, and an old, floppy sailor cap. He carried a fishing pool, a sack lunch, and an oversized tackle box. Tucked into his belt, under his shirt was his silenced automatic pistol with its high-capacity clip. Out of deference to his neighbors, he closed his apartment door without a sound and walked as silently as possible down to the parking lot. It took a minute to hitch his boat trailer to his car. If anyone was watching, Mierie looked like he was on his way to a quiet morning of fishing on the river.

*****

At 6:35, right on cue, Alex crossed the short space between the concealing cluster of pipes and entered the Penetration Access Hallway. He kept a wary eye for Brian as he swiped his badge and entered the Penetration Access Hallway. No alarms went off and he began to feel a little more secure. He quick-stepped the short distance to door of PSB-34 and swiped his ID card.

*****

A few seconds later, Manuel reset Minerva Hopkins's personnel ID number.

*****

As Alex was going through door PSB-34, Brian opened the Maintenance Building emergency exit. As the door opened, it blocked Brian's view of the parking lot. Brian did, however, have a clear view of the access road leading to the River Water Pump House. The road was empty, and no one was visible at the pump house in the distance. Brian stepped around the door and scanned the parking lot. It was daylight, so Brian could see the entire parking lot clearly. A couple of cars were entering the parking lot and several people walked in from the parking lot, but no Mr. Cargo Vest.

In a flash, Brian spun and reached out, but the Maintenance Building exit door had clicked shut behind him. Brian looked at the door in resigned anger, and breathed a single, slow breath of exasperation. He turned and walked along the face of the building, intending to reenter the building using the Turbine Building access door. But, as he approached the access door, he decided to walk around to the front of the building to the main personnel entrance instead. Brian had about twenty minutes to file a quick security report and get to the conference room. He wasn't going to miss that call. After all, a temporary employee stealing hardware from the plant was a security problem, not an operations problem. Security could find and question Mr. Cargo Vest.

*****

As Brian passed the Turbine Building exit, Manuel changed Callum Holman's personnel ID number to match the selected contraband badge.

*****

A few moments later, as Brian entered the front door of the administration wing, Alex James entered Cable Penetration Room 24. It was 6:40.

*****

After the program logged the door entry record for CPR-24, Manuel restored Callum Holman's personnel ID number. Manuel knew that he had about twenty-five minutes before he had to make another ID change, so he decided to go down to the coffee shop on the ground floor and see if there was any buzz about anything going on at Desert Canyons. The hallways were filling up. There was a lot of buzz, but it was all about the refueling shutdown. Everything was almost too normal.

*****

Everything at the power plant was humming along with a familiar background song. Everything seemed normal to Alex James as he stepped into the cable penetration room. It did not register that the temperature in the room was over a hundred degrees. There wasn't enough daily traffic to warrant air conditioning in the room. It also didn't register that there was a considerable background radiation in the room because of its proximity to the nuclear reactor, fifteen feet away, beyond the curved wall of the Containment Vessel. There was no need for a permanent Radiation Control Point. If someone needed to enter the room for work, a RADCON tech could install a temporary RCP in two hours.

The penetration room was unusual. It was fifteen feet wide on the side closest to containment, and sixteen-and-a-half feet at the side farthest from containment. This made the room wedge-shaped toward the rounded wall of the Containment Vessel. The room was twenty-two feet long and had twelve-foot ceilings. The walls, floor, and ceiling were featureless, unfinished, concrete slabs. There was one door and no windows in the cell. The cable-sorting trays stacked like shelves along both walls. The trays themselves looked like ladders that were laid on their sides. Individual cables entered the room through the wall farthest from the containment wall and routed onto a cable-routing tray and to the appropriate penetration. Once electricians connected a cable to a penetration, the circuit disappeared into containment.

For Alex, the horizontal cable trays formed a sort of ladder. He climbed up the sides to the right place, swung back to a sitting position on an adjacent tray, and went to work. If someone entered the room, Alex had only to turn to the side, lean back, and lie down to be invisible from the floor. The maze of trays and cables concealed the trigger box.

Alex went to work. He found cable PCRV-1254C, and used a pair of wire cutters to cut away the woven, copper armor. Next, he used a small, curved box cutter with the blade exposed to the exact thickness of the heavy-duty, plastic outer insulation to slice, and removed twelve inches of the outer insulation without damaging the delicate individual wires inside. With the outer cover removed, he had exposed a couple of dozen individually insulated wires. Alex used an electric wire stripper that looked like a pair of pliers with holes drilled in the jaws instead of grooves, to remove the insulation from the ground wire. Alex closed the jaws on the ground wire and pushed the heater button. After a second, he slid the strippers down the conductor. The heated jaws melted the insulation away like candle wax, but they were not hot enough to melt the metal wire inside. He exposed six inches of the shiny wire and connected the ground wire from the trigger box. Alex worked with practiced precision, even though he was a nervous wreck. While he worked, Alex again began to remember.

*****

While Alex worked, Brian walked into the Personnel Access Center at the front of the Administration Building. To the right were the four metal detector portals with a small conveyor belt running alongside. Guards monitored the metal detectors, checked badges, and searched hand-carried items for the steady stream of employees. To the left, the watch commander sat at a shorter length of counter.

Brian stepped up to the counter and waited for the watch commander to notice him. The man looked like an ex-Marine who could handle about any situation. He was in uniform, had a gun, and was obviously busy. Brian waited. After a few seconds, the watch commander looked up and smiled.

"Yes, Sir, may I help you?" the watch commander asked. He was the picture of accommodation and service.

"Yes, thank you." Brian said. "I believe that I have seen one of our temporary employees stealing materials from the plant. I know that he was in areas which he shouldn't have had access." Brian described Mr. Cargo Vest and related the incident in

The Commons. The watch commander wrote it all down. Brian told the commander about seeing Mr. Cargo Vest at the equipment rack in the high bay and following him to the ground floor where he lost him. The watch commander also wrote down the details of the midnight encounter at the Maintenance Building exit a few nights ago. A picture was beginning to emerge.

"One last thing," Brian said, "Lenell Spector has been tracking some bogus entries in the door access logs for the past couple of weeks. When we compared notes, it looked like this may have been the same man. You might talk to her, as well."

"What was that name, again?"

"Lenell Spector."

"Excellent," said the commander, "Anything else?"

"No, I think that's it."

"Sign here. I'll have someone watch the surveillance cameras and see if we can pick up Mr. Cargo Vest, cute name. I'll also notify the entire shift to be on the lookout for him."

"Do your surveillance cameras record?" Brian asked.

"Unfortunately, no. The system's new in the last few weeks and the recorders are glitchy at best."

Brian left the main personnel entrance and walked toward the conference room. His conference call would start any minute now.

*****

At two minutes to seven, Alex made his final connections. Most of the time, he focused on task. While his hands were performing the memorized steps, Alex's mind drifted to exploding brick, sparkling glass, and red dust. A giraffe could have walked across the floor and Alex wouldn't have seen it. It didn't register to Alex that Solenoid Valve A had changed position and back when he cut and reconnected the hot wire. It also did not register that the indicator light for Solenoid Valve C showed that the valve changed position when he cut the hot wire, but that the valve didn't return to its normal position when he reconnected the permanent wire to the hot wire from the trigger box. Solenoid Valve C got stuck somewhere between full-open and full-closed. The operation of Solenoid Valve C was now *unpredictable*. Air was leaking out, but no air came back in.

Chapter Twelve

At seven sharp, Brian walked into the conference room. A tech was waiting for him and said, "Good morning, Brian. One moment, and I'll log you in." The tech typed in an authorization code and introduced Brian to those already in attendance. The conference host welcomed Brian, and the various conversations continued. After a few minutes of preliminary discussions, Brian had the tech mute his microphone and he made some notes. This was going to be a long, painfully slow process. It confirmed Brian's opinion that meetings were the superglue that lubricated the wheels of progress.

*****

Also, at seven sharp, Mierie arrived at the boat ramp and launched his fishing boat. No one else was there. Things were going well.

*****

As Mierie's boat touched the water, Dax explained the features of the small emergency diesel generator at the River Water Pump House to his student. The diluted contaminated liquid waste continued to discharge into the river.

*****

In the control room, Downing asked his control room operator to page Warder Alan, the floor operator, and ask him to come to the control room. Air Compressor B chose that moment to auto-start and top off the compressed air storage tank. As the control room operator pressed the page key on his phone, the Air Compressor B Auto-Start alarm sounded. Most of the people on the floor at the plant heard the muffled, semi-intelligible message, "Warder Alan, call the control room. Warder Alan, call the control room." Everyone heard the strident urgency of the Air Compressor B Alarm in the background of the announcement.

*****

Alex ran the trigger-phone cable around the outside edge of the penetration room and connected it to the computer receptacle by the door. He was climbing back up the cable trays to collect his tools, when he heard the garbled message and background alarm broadcast over the PA system. He almost jumped out of his skin. He didn't know that the alarm was routine. He didn't know who Warder Alan was. He collected his tools, jumped down from the stack of cable trays, and started to walk toward the door. He wondered why the alarms were sounding. *Has something gone wrong?* He began to panic. He was sweating and gasping.

Alex felt like he'd been punched in the chest from all sides at once. He didn't realize that the origin of the blow came from inside. All of Alex's air went out of his lungs in one gasp and he couldn't pull it back in. He couldn't breathe. He tried to scream but made no sound. All focus on the script dissolved. His arms hung at his sides like two sacks of sand. He felt a hundred pairs of vise-grip pliers reach into his chest and take hold of a separate, exposed nerve. The grip in his chest squeezed and squeezed. He couldn't think about anything except the pain; it was as cold as arctic sleet and needle sharp. Little explosions of white light flashed in his eyes, and terror washed over him. As he sank to his knees, his hearing faded to a dull roar. The world contracted to a small picture at the end of a long, black tunnel. It felt to Alex as if the pairs of pliers in his chest had begun to twist, slow and relentless. He couldn't breathe, and the world around him began to fade. In exaggerated slow motion, he pitched forward. His last conscious thought was that he had now failed at the one task Allah had set before him. Alex James, Adawi Aimur-Noor, the Son of the Lion, a son of Egypt, was dead before his face hit the floor. It was five minutes after seven.

*****

As Alex was dying, Lenell was leaving her condominium. She was forty-five minutes earlier than normal so she could catch Brian between his teleconference and the start of his shift. Once he was on shift, he would be unavailable for the rest of the day. She was determined not to miss the opportunity to see him for a few minutes.

*****

Per the script, at 7:08, Manuel walked back into his office, sat down at his desk, and made the ID changes for Callum Holman that would allow Alex to exit the cable penetration room. He waited for the log entry to signal that Alex had left the room. 7:10 came and went. 7:12 came and went. Where was Alex? Why hadn't he left the cable penetration room? By 7:15, Alex hadn't exited the cable penetration room, nor had he entered the piping penetration room. *Something must have gone wrong.*

Manuel began to panic a little, then a lot. Manuel concocted every conceivable, paranoid scenario possible. Did the authorities know about the plot all along? Were they coming to arrest him right now? Maybe someone discovered Alex installing the trigger box, and he was hiding. Manuel had the sinking feeling that he would never see a penny of his offshore nest egg. He watched his computer for the telltale entries that would show him what was going on. Over the next fifteen minutes, depression set in. Manuel believed that he could count his life of freedom in minutes and seconds. His bluster and bravado turned to fear and isolation. He sweated heavily. He waited for the authorities to come busting into his office and throw him to the floor. He was morbidly afraid of experiencing pain in the takedown. He was already practicing how he would scream like a little girl, "Don't hurt me. Don't hurt me." He didn't know what else to do, so he waited.

*****

At Desert Canyons, the air continued to bleed from the Relief Valve C reservoir.

*****

As Manuel stewed in his own fear, Lenell arrived at the plant. She passed through security without incident and walked up to her office with a little extra kick in her step. It was a beautiful morning. She wanted to know if there were any unauthorized entries this morning, so she ordered a copy of the access report for the last twenty-four hours. She watched the printer process the report and took a quick look to make sure that it covered the right time. Then, she sat back down. As an afterthought, she requested a copy of the door access report from the night of the 22nd. She'd look at them later.

She scoured the report for the 22nd, and, yes, there was a bogus entry for the Maintenance Building emergency exit at midnight on the 22nd.

"There it is!" Over the next few minutes, Lenell identified several other impossible entries. Most were for people who weren't in the plant on the 22nd. At least one of the entries was for someone who wasn't even in California on the 22nd.

Lenell had missed catching Brian before his conference, so she worked on her computer report as Brian listened to his phone. In the control room, Downing prepared for shift change. Air continued to bleed from the relief valve actuator. The air pressure in the actuator was approaching the minimum pressure needed to keep the relief valve closed and sealed. The primary coolant relief valve started to bleed primary cooling water out of the primary coolant system.

The high pressure of the primary coolant system allowed the normal operating temperature of the water in a primary coolant system to increase to six hundred and forty degrees, far above the normal boiling temperature for water at atmospheric pressure. High pressure kept the water in liquid form, much like the water in a pressurized automobile radiator. When the superheated water seeped through the valve seals, the pressure was relieved, and the superheated water flashed to steam. The resulting steam contacted the cool inside surface of the downspout piping where it re-condensed into water. The downspout pipe routed the water to the containment sump which had temperature, moisture, and water level indicators.

There was a procedure for what to do if the relief valves opened during normal operations (lots of water in the containment sump.) There was a procedure for what to do if the relief valves closed (no water in the containment sump), but there was no procedure for what to do if the relief valve stuck somewhere in between open and closed (some water in the containment sump.) The closest reference was a procedure that said that a little bit of water was from some other system like the air conditioning or a leaky seal on one of the primary cooling water make-up water pumps.

*****

In the control room, Operations Shift Supervisor Downing noticed the slight increase in temperature and moisture in the containment sump. He verified that there was no change in the primary coolant system temperature or pressure. He also noticed that Primary Cooling Water Make-up Pump B was running.

The running primary cooling water make-up pumps must be losing a shaft water seal, Downing thought, true to his training. However, his shift would end in less than twenty minutes. The schedule has the *day shift shutting down the plant anyway. Let them worry about the leaky seal.* He reached over and bypassed the Primary Cooling Water Make-up Pumps. He didn't announce the operation because he didn't want to make a log entry and be stuck explaining himself for another hour. Again, let the golden boy on day shift worry about it.

Chapter Thirteen

At fifteen minutes to eight, Brian's control room operator, Christina Belvoir, walked into the control room and scanned the various meters and gauges. She was more than a little excited about being the control room operator who would perform the plant shutdown. She'd never even seen a nuclear power plant shutdown. She told everyone that she'd arrived early because she wanted to get the turnover 'exercise' out of the way before the control room got too chaotic, but secretly, she'd been anxious to take control and be *in charge*.

The outgoing control room operator (nicknamed 'Dense David') seemed to be dragging his feet. She thought that he seemed to want to stay in the control room as long as possible. She wanted to look him in the eye and say, "Get out," but she didn't. Downing was monitoring the plant, so she relaxed.

This is going to be an exciting day, she thought. She was anticipating being in the limelight as the control room operator selected to shut the power plant down.

*****

At a quarter to eight, Lenell walked out of her ground floor office with the computer printouts in hand. She had time to catch Brian between the conference room and the control room and show him the printouts. Her door clicked shut behind her, and she turned toward the elevators. She looked up and recognized the plant manager and two security guards walking toward her.

"Lenell," Smithson called to her, "may I have a moment?"

Lenell walked down to meet them at the elevator. "Good morning, Jack," she said.

"Good morning," Jack Smithson smiled. "Look, I only have a second. I'm on my way up to watch the festivities in the control room. Here's the short of it, your boss finally pulled the plug. He resigned. We've been in legal wrangling with him for weeks. We also suspected him of being behind the string of computer access problems that we've had over the last few weeks. He's in the process of separating from the utility to work for an anti-nuclear environmental group. Legal hasn't allowed me to say a word to anyone. The formal announcement will come out later this morning. This is going to open a management position, and I want you to submit for consideration. People have been watching your work. We all consider you 'the candidate.' Get your resume together and see Mattie at your first opportunity. She'll have the details. I don't want this to wait. Come by my office in the morning and we'll talk …Lenell!" When Lenell didn't respond, Smithson raised his brows and waited for his words to sink in.

Lenell was surprised into silence. "Uh…Uh…yes. I'll see you in the morning." She looked at Smithson, then at the security guards, and then back at Smithson. "Uh, Jack, you needed a security guard escort to back you up to tell me this?"

"They aren't with me," he said, pleased with himself. "They're looking for someone called Mr. Cargo Vest and they want to talk to Brian. I'll see you tomorrow."

The elevator door opened. Jack and the security guards stepped in. The door closed. Lenell stared at the closed elevator door as if it would provide more explanation. She had forgotten where she was going.

When she gathered her wits about her, she reached up and pushed the up arrow again. She needed the elevator ride to regain some of her composure.

*****

As Lenell composed herself in the elevator, Mierie parked his car and trailer at the boat ramp parking spot. He'd already launched the boat and moored it at the end of the launching dock. Mierie whistled as though he didn't have a worry in the world as he walked to his boat.

*****

At that instant in the reactor core, small steam bubbles began to form around the hottest spots in the core. They were short-lived and non-intrusive. Near the reactor core, the cascading bubbles sounded like wooden marbles in a metal can. The whisper of metal getting too hot was too faint.

*****

The elevator door opened before Lenell was ready, and she found herself face-to-face with Brian Sing.

"Oh, Brian, good morning! I am so glad I ran into you! I reprinted the door-open report for the 22nd. You were right; there was a bogus entry at the Maintenance Building exit. I also found several other bogus entries on the night. It looks like the *bogie* wandered all over the plant that night," she said in a rush.

"I knew it. I'm due in the control room right now, but I need you to do something for me. I saw our mystery man in the plant this morning between six and seven. I lost him on the ground floor of the Turbine Building high bay. I think he was stealing equipment off the high bay shelves. Run a report for this morning, six to seven, and see if the bogus entries can tell us what doors he accessed. Oh, and please, bring the report up to me in the control room when you can. I gotta run. Bye."

"I will," Lenell answered. With that, Brian was gone. Lenell felt a little put off by Brian being so abrupt. She wanted a little more personal interaction and would have liked knowing how much her presence had affected Brian.

As Brian stepped into the control room, he found himself looking over the shoulders of two security guards at a large assembly of dignitaries in the conference room. They were chatting and laughing amongst themselves. None of them noticed the drama in the control room.

"Mr. Sing?"

"Yes."

"May we have a minute of your time before you get too busy?"

The older guard asked. "Big day, huh?" he added.

Brian figured that this was about Mr. Cargo Vest. He stepped to the side, prepared to answer a few questions, and said, "Of course." Brian did not have a couple of minutes.

*****

At 7:48 a.m., Mierie left the boat ramp for the leisurely boat trip up the river.

*****

Three long, slow minutes went by. Downing was still standing at the control console watching the conditions in the primary system deteriorate. He could see Sing standing at the back of the control room talking to a couple of security guards. *Come on, Sing,* he thought with mounting exasperation, *It's time for shift change. Let's get this show on the road.* Downing looked down at the containment sump temperature indicators. *Come on, Sing,* he mouthed to himself.

More steam was seeping through the seat of the relief valve. The high pressure and temperature steam was now cutting its own channel through the stainless-steel valve seat. More superheated water meant more superheated steam and hotter condensate. The sump water level transmitter registered a slight rise in water level. The temperature was rising as well. Downing saw more fluctuations in the reactor conditions. He was feeling more uneasy than ever.

Come on, Sing, it's time for shift change.

That's when Downing did something rash, destructively rash. He reached up and turned the Scram Auto/Bypass selector switch to 'Bypass.' It was a moment of pure self-preservation, and Josef would have been proud.

During normal operations, the Scram Auto/Bypass selector switch was in the 'Auto' position. If there were too many unexplained fluctuations in the operation of the reactor, the 'Auto' circuit shut down the reactor, but during the startup and shutdown of the reactor, fluctuations in pressure and temperature were unavoidable. An operator would seldom complete a reactor startup without the option to bypass the Auto Scram circuit.

Downing wouldn't allow an automatic Scram in the last few minutes of his last shift to ruin his week.

He had been considering retiring for some time because he was having some trouble handling the stress of the job. Having the reactor act up this morning was almost more than he could handle. He was desperate to make a clean getaway from the control room this morning. He wanted the reactor to hang together for just a few more minutes, and he would be out of there.

At the moment he turned the Bypass switch, the control room went silent. Everyone in the conference was engaged in conversation. The two security guards focused on Brian Sing and wouldn't have realized what they saw if they had seen it. Sing was facing away from the reactor control console and didn't see anything. Christina was facing Dense David and trying to concentrate on his extended litany of turnover facts.

Dense David, however, was looking at Downing with more than a distracted anticipation. In fact, he focused on Downing with an almost-obsessive intensity. Dense David saw Downing turn the Bypass switch and knew what it meant for Desert Canyons. He froze for a moment. He could not believe his eyes or his good fortune. Downing had done David's job for him. Downing had turned the switch. David didn't have to turn the switch. No one could blame David for the Bypass switch being in the wrong position. David was in the clear.

A few weeks before, a man had approached Dense David and offered to pay his accumulated gambling debt in cash in exchange for one, small, insignificant action in the control room. Josef was certain that Downing would turn the Auto Scram Bypass Switch to Bypass, but he left as little as possible to chance. If Downing didn't panic and bypass the Auto Scram, Dense David would.

But Downing did bypass the Auto Scram function. No one outside of the control room would ever know who flipped the switch. That odd little man would have no way to verify that it wasn't Dense David who turned the switch. Dense David's gambling debts evaporated. He was in the clear. As the wave of relief subsided, he vowed to never get into debt with a bookie again. No, in the future, he would restrict his betting to a *sure thing.* He could tell the difference and restrain himself. He was the picture of self-control. No more high-risk bets. He finished the turnover process with Christina and turned to leave the control room. As he walked out, he wondered if there was any good college basketball action tonight. He felt good.

As Dense David left the control room, Lenell reentered her office and looked at the printout of the door-open requests for that morning. She planned to compare the names to her printout from the 22nd and see if any were the same. She would also look for new, out-of-place, names, but that might take a while. Maybe she should update her resume first. An assignment to a management position trumped finding a petty thief any day. Brian would be busy all morning anyway. Lenell sat down to her computer and opened her current resume file.

*****

At his office downtown, Manuel Rojas was giving himself a heart attack. He had been watching the minute-to-minute activity in the door authorization database. Alex James went into CPR-24 but didn't come out. He couldn't contact Josef or Mierie for instructions, so he just sat and stewed. Everything was wrong. *They must be onto the plot at Desert Canyons.* There was no other explanation. His first impulse was to race to the airport to get away, but Josef had told him to be patient. Josef said that to run would most assuredly focus the suspicion of guilt on him. Besides, Alex James might reappear on the request data stream. Without Manuel to clear the way, the Door Security System would trap Alex James in CPR-24. He had to wait. Besides, he believed that there was no way for the authorities to connect him to the un-authorized data changes. He changed all the ID numbers back to normal. Then, with considerable effort, he forced himself to sit down at his desk and go back to work. He was, however, hyper-vigilant to all the activity around him. He was dying the pro-verbial slow death inside.

*****

Josef, on the other hand, was touring an eighteenth-century antebel-lum plantation house on the banks of the Mississippi River outside New Orleans. He had just entered a small tourist café for a glass of iced tea. He absently wondered if the events at Desert Canyons were unfolding as planned. Iced tea sounded refreshing.

Chapter Fourteen

In the moment before chaos, there is a moment of pure peace. 7:54 a.m. PST was such a moment. At the Cyprus Lane antebellum house in Louisiana, Josef took a sip of sweet tea. On the river, Mierie relished the rush of cool wind in his face as his boat glided upstream. In the downtown office, Manuel resigned himself to the fates and found an inner peace. In the Desert Canyons control room, Downing knew that his struggle to keep up with the technology of the nuclear power industry was over; he would retire. Outside the control room, Dense David remembered a good basketball game scheduled for that night, a *sure thing*. Christina owned the control room. Dax was at the River Water Pump House talking about the Water Strainer Blowdown System. In her office, Lenell was preparing her resume. Brian turned to the control room: he was in his element. The world was as it should be.

At 7:55 a.m., PST, the weakened air charge on Primary Coolant Relief Valve C could no longer hold the primary coolant relief valve closed. With a shudder and a loud bang, the spring-loaded relief valve slammed open with a staggering level of violence. It had the full twenty-two hundred pounds of pressure of the Primary Cooling Water System behind it.

*****

By standard procedure, operators would shut down a nuclear power over several hours or days to allow the super-heated components time to equalize to ambient temperatures. Control rods would be inserted slowly to supply a slow temperature transition in the nuclear fuel. Even with the control rods inserted after prolonged periods of full power operations, it could take days for the residual nuclear reactions to decay. It could take even longer for the heat produced by these reactions to be wicked away by the Primary Cooling Water System. The high rate of nuclear reactions could not just stop, nor could the high rate of heat production. It would be like stopping the flow of heat from volcanic lava. Just because the lava stopped moving doesn't mean that it would be cool to the touch and does not mean that the lava would be safe.

Primary Coolant Relief Valve C at the Desert Canyons nuclear power plant overcame the air pressure and spring pressure designed to keep it closed. It snapped open, exposing the high pressure and high temperature primary cooling water to the low-pressure atmosphere of the Containment Vessel.

*****

Christina noticed it first. In a split second, she saw and recognized the flashing of the "Liquid Water in the Containment Sump" alarm. She partially inhaled once.

In the first seconds, there was a sudden loss of pressure in the reactor, like popping the pressurized radiator cap on an overheated late model car, only a hundred times more violent. Pockets of superheated water flashed to superheated steam in a process called nucleate boiling. As the size of the bubbles increased, the force of the exploding bubbles pushed the surrounding water away with a tremendously destructive force called water hammer. At those temperatures and pressures, it was more like water sledgehammer. The metal fuel rods and supporting structures in the reactor bent and broken like aluminum foil hats. Inside the steam bubbles, there was nowhere for the excess reactor heat to go. It built up quickly, overheating the surrounding metal. The expelled steam cooled, condensed back to water, and rushed back into the void. The cooled water hit the superheated metal and the cycle started anew. The catastrophic forces at play would render the reactor's internal structures unrecognizable. Warping structural materials breached fuel rods. Fission products and reactor debris flooded the water/steam mix. The water, steam, and nuclear waste gushed out through the open relief valve like rusty water from a radiator. The Reactor Scram Bypass switch was in Bypass. The reactor had not scrammed, and the control rods had not inserted. Heat and radiation production continued whenever water was present to moderate the nuclear process. Flooding a super-heated nuclear reactor with cold moderating water was like throwing liquid gasoline on a campfire.

The make-up pumps were off. No make-up water was entering the reactor, so the periodic tide of cooling water returning to the reactor became less and less frequent. Too much heat and radiation caused most of the internal metal structure to thermally fatigue. Thermal fatigue made some components brittle, and they shattered like glass. Thermal fatigue caused other components to lose strength and become porous. They dissolved like sugar cubes. The slurry of melted metals cooled and congealed back to a solid metal whenever it flowed over the cooler metals below it.

Throughout the entire process, the various nuclear and chemical reactions gave off a variety of gases like nitrogen, helium, argon, and, most especially, hydrogen. The whole reactor was a mass of rolling, boiling bubbles, water hammer, disintegrating metals, and radioactive debris waiting for some outside force to deliver the final destructive blow. In tiny amounts, hydrogen built up in the highest reaches of the Containment Vessel. Desert Canyons was dying.

*****

The morning was quiet on the river opposite the power station as Mierie positioned his boat to make it look like he was fishing. It was eight o'clock. Mierie watched for Alex James to step out onto the observation deck. All was calm.

*****

Christina saw the "Liquid Water in the Containment Sump" alarm light up. She was about to announce the new alarm when half the alarms in the control room lit up at one time. The main turbine steam isolation valves closed, the distribution breakers for the main generator opened, the regular lights throughout the power plant went out, and the emergency lights came on. Automated announcements started broadcasting.

Christina started announcing the new alarms as fast as she could, "Containment Sump High Water Level."

"Reactor Coolant Low Pressure."

"Reactor Local Temperature Multiple Sensors High."

"Main Generator Feeder Breakers Open."

"Hotel Electric Supply Breakers Closed."

"Diesels One and Two Auto-Start."

"Fission Products in the Containment Vessel."

Christina turned to look at Downing. He stood stone still and stared at the reactor control console. His face was slack, and he didn't seem to be breathing. Full-blown sensory overload froze him to inactivity. Christina turned to Brian, who stepped around the security guards.

She shouted in a panicked voice, "Brian, we have both 'Loss of Coolant' and 'Breach of Fuel Integrity' alarms. Downing's lost it. Do something!"

Brian stepped up next to Downing and demanded, "Downing, what happened?" For a second, Downing didn't move. Then, like a parody of a slow-motion movie, he turned to look in Brian's direction. Brian was not sure that Downing could see him.

"I'm taking the control room. Somebody take Downing over there and sit him down." Brian announced.

Brian turned back to the console, "Christina, announce that the reactor has scrammed, that the turbine has tripped, and that the main generator feeder breaker opened. Check the diesel generators. And somebody silence that auto announcement!"

The public address broadcast alerted the floor operators of the plant status and notified them that they must now perform several associated emergency shutdown operations. The floor operators jumped like their feet were on fire and began performing the required emergency shutdown procedures.

Christina silenced the "Turbine Trip Alarm." When the primary coolant system lost pressure, the steam generators quit making steam. When the flow of steam to the main turbine-generator dramatically reduced, the main generator quit being a giant generator and tried to become a giant motor. Motorizing the main generator pulled electrical power from the main electrical power grid so Desert Canyons would no longer be a supplier of electricity; instead, it would be a huge consumer. An automatic circuit ensured that this didn't happen. The Main Generator Reverse Power relay 'Tripped' and the feeder breakers opened. At least one thing had gone right.

Christina was making announcements when she noticed that the control rods had not inserted. With a start, she realized that she hadn't heard the 'Reactor has Scrammed' announcement. She screamed in panic this time, "Brian, the reactor didn't Scram!" She reached for the Scram button before she finished her sentence.

Brian checked his board. The control rods were still in the normal operating position. The Scram Bypass Switch was set to Bypass. "Christina, Scram the reactor! Scram the reactor!" Brian ordered.

Christina pushed the Scram button. Brian turned the Scram Bypass Switch to Auto. Later, he would remember that the reactor hadn't scrammed, but he wouldn't remember turning the switch back to "Auto."

During a normal emergency shutdown, hydraulic motors pushed the 236 stainless-steel control rods into the reactor from above. If the hydraulics failed, gravity assisted the insertion process. On this day, the hydraulic system began pushing the control rods into the reactor. Some of the control rods inserted all the way to the bottom, squelching the nuclear fission in the immediate area of the inserted rods. Most, however, met some resistance. These control rods knifed through as much structural material as possible before becoming part of the damage. They also cut into more of the warped and bent fuel rods. At this instant, shutting down the fission process was more important than minimizing structural damage. After the *accident*, it would be determined that over half of the reactor internal structure had melted, and that ninety percent of the fuel rods had breached.

Brian stepped back to the shift supervisor's desk. He had a "Loss of Coolant Accident" combined with a "Fuel Rod Breach." He didn't know the extent of the internal damage. He did know that radioactive contamination was coursing into the Containment Vessel. There was nothing to indicate radioactive contamination in the plant proper. Protecting people always came first. He reached down and pushed the "Plant Emergency Evacuation" button.

An automated voice announced across all plant intercoms and to all plant phones that there was a "Class One Nuclear Evacuation."

Everyone in Desert Canyons who was not required for the safe operation of Desert Canyons was ordered to evacuate to the Safe Staging Area, the remote parking lot out by the turnoff from the main highway. The first priority was to get the staff as far from the plant as was practical to ensure that they wouldn't be further contaminated, but not so far away that they would further spread existing contamination, if there was any.

Brian spun around to Jack Smithson, and ordered his boss to, "Get those people out of here and to the staging area, and then come back." He didn't wait for a response.

Brian spun back to the reactor control console. *Why isn't the reactor beginning to cool down,* he asked himself. That was when he looked at the three primary coolant make-up pumps and saw that they were off.

"Christina, why are the PCMU pumps off?" he called.

"I didn't know that the PCMU pumps were offline," she responded.

"Starting PCMU pumps one, two, and three." He turned all three PCMU pumps on. In the reactor, a gush of frigid water hit the 2000-degree tangled mass of structural materials, and the process started again. Steam bubbles formed. Radioactive debris and waste churned into the water, and then the high pressure forced the water out through the relief valve. It was necessary. Operators were further cooling the reactor at the expense of spreading radioactive waste to every interior surface in the Containment Vessel. The Containment Vessel maintained its integrity, and no radioactive waste escaped from it. Inside the Containment Vessel, the accident was coating the once pristine white structure and stainless-steel equipment with mucky nuclear waste. The once super-clean primary cooling water system now looked like a swimming pool with a dump truck of fireplace ashes dumped into it.

Brian's skin began to crawl. He could almost feel the damage that the cold water was causing in the reactor. He forced himself to take long, deep breaths. He imagined that he could smell and taste the pollution in, and the damage to, his beloved power plant. The reactor was not shutting down fast enough. He knew what he had to do but didn't want to admit this level of defeat and take the steps to permanently shut down the runaway nuclear mess.

"Initiating boron injection," he announced. He pressed the boron injection button. In a room high above the main reactor, a series of valves opened, and high-pressure water began to flow unimpeded into the reactor itself. The water contained a thick chemical compound of boric acid and emulsifiers. The boron absorbed neutrons like a sponge. Without neutrons, the reactor couldn't react. It was like covering a dumpster fire with the contents of an airport runway foam suppression truck. The boric acid and emulsifiers squelched the remaining nuclear cascade.

Brian had been on shift for twenty-five minutes. It had been less than an hour since the air solenoid valve for Primary Coolant Relief

Valve C had stuck halfway open. Six hundred gallons of borated water had completed the emergency shutdown of Desert Canyons Nuclear Power Station. The temperatures in the reactor began to decrease slightly because enough cooling water was getting into the core. The temperatures and water levels became more stable, and the steam pockets and bubbles subsided. In less than an hour, Desert Canyons had gone from being one of this country's premier examples of high-tech electrical power production to being the world's largest radioactive paperweight. Brian Sing leaned forward, put his palms on the reactor control console, took a deep breath, closed his eyes, and bowed his head in disbelief. For now, the threat of a nuclear contamination release to the environment of Southern California was almost over.

When the first announcements were broadcast, Downing and Sing's senior floor operators stopped mid-turnover and went to the main turbine deck. With a loss of coolant and a class one evacuation, both knew that neither would be going home soon. Their job was to monitor the shutdown of the main turbine-generator. If the floor operators allowed the main turbine-generator to spin down and stop while it was still at operating temperature, the generator's shaft would bow like a wet noodle. Shaft-driven bearing oil and bearing cooling water pumps would spin down and stop. The hot bearings would seize. To prevent this damage to the turbine-generator, the operators started the electric bearing oil and bearing cooling water pumps. They also watched the turning rate. The turning rate during operations was 1850 revolutions per minute. At sixty RPM (one revolution per second), the gear of an electric turning motor was engaged. The turbine-generator turned at sixty RPM for hours or days until the main shaft cooled to room temperature.

On the Turbine Building floor, the junior floor operators worked together to safely shutdown a myriad of secondary equipment. The Demineralized Water Still was already in hot standby. One operator placed the steam-driven feed water pumps in hot standby. The other checked on the operation of three diesel generators. Both watched for stray staff members who might need reminding that the evacuation was mandatory.

They all checked every radiation monitor they passed for elevated radiation levels. All four operators would be busy for the rest of the day.

*****

At the River Water Pump House, Dax saw the telltale blink of the lights. He had already shut down the liquid waste discharge. His silence and demeanor told Donny to keep quiet. They were exiting the River Water Pump House when the announcements came. He had originnally planned to take Donny to the control room first and let him see the excitement. As far as Dax knew, the reactor had 'scrammed' as part of a normal routine. Just another day at work.

Dax stopped walking and listened to the announcements. Upon hearing the mandatory evacuation announcement, he decided to skirt the building and take his student to the main gate for evacuation. Dax was so focused that he wouldn't have heard the student speak even if he had spoken. Once the student was safe, Dax would return to the control room. Dax was *essential personnel*.

*****

From his fishing boat, Mierie heard the initial announcements.

Good, it has started, he thought to himself. He was tired of waiting and pretending. The evacuation alarm confirmed his assumption. They had succeeded.

"Praise be to Allah," he said aloud.

That was when he saw Dax and the student walking up the hill. He stood up to get a better look. They were supposed to be dead. He snapped around to look at the observation deck. *Where is Alex?* he asked himself. *The destruction of Desert Canyons has started, for sure.* That was obvious. But where was Alex James?

Mierie wondered if pollution was spewing into the river. Alex was not where he was supposed to be. Some part of the plan had failed. *Did they catch him? Is he talking right now?*

Mierie slowly put his fishing gear away, sat down, and started the boat's motor. He turned the boat around and putted slowly downriver toward the boat ramp. Every now and again, he dropped a piece of the gun or hardware into the river. About halfway back to the boat launch, he waved down another boat that was moving upstream.

"Might not want to go up there," he said like any other good citizen doing a good deed. "A lot of alarms are going off at Desert Canyons." After a quick wave, Mierie moved on. The other boat turned around.

Where was Alex James?

*****

Jack Smithson was standing in the conference room when the first alarm sounded. He moved to the open door, knowing that this wasn't the planned shutdown scenario. An automated voice announced, "Class One Nuclear Evacuation" to the people in the conference room.

Oh, crap, he thought, but Brian turned to him and stopped his thought.

"Get those people out of here!" Brian ordered. His facial expression and voice left no doubt that it was a direct order. Smithson turned back to the gaggle of managers staring at him and told them to follow him to the main gate. After they merged his group with the mob of people headed out; Smithson turned and went back in. He, too, was *essential personnel*.

*****

The mob of evacuees rushed through the main security gate. The guards confiscated all hand-carried objects, except for purses. The employees also left their hats and coats in the guard shack. If radioactive contamination in the form of dust escaped the Containment Vessel it would have settled on the tops of hats, the shoulders of coats, and on any other object that happened to be in the room. Radioactive debris also tended to rub off onto any object that touched a contaminated surface. Plant security officers didn't allow anyone to return to their cars. With an impromptu security escort, the main mass of the employees walked to the remote parking lot a half mile or so up the access road.

A dozen security people had already arrived and were busy setting up pop-up canopy covers for shade. People unloaded chairs and drinking-water stations every few feet. A variety of food, including doughnuts and cold cuts arrived. These weren't refugees of a war; they were nuclear power plant staff worthy of respect and consideration. One of the female document center managers complained of a tightness in her chest, so she was the first one scanned for radioactive contamination and cleared. One of the guards used a security vehicle to take her to the hospital.

Also in the group at the remote parking lot was a small army of Health Physics staff. HPs were responsible for monitoring and mitigating the spread of nuclear contamination. They set up walk-through portals and started directing staff members to walk through them. They used hand-held monitors to scan the people's feet, hands, and faces.

After HP's deemed an individual free of contamination, they released the individual to the other side of the parking lot where security staff checked their IDs, photographed them, and took statements. Processed and released staff stepped into the remote parking guard shack and called home to have a relative or friend come out and pick them up. Others took a cold drink, sat down in the shade of a canopy, and waited for the busses to arrive.

As the local HPs worked the crowd, a small army of HPs, some from other facilities, descended upon Desert Canyons. They sampled the air, the water, and the dust. They set up radiation monitors on roof drains, vents, gutters, sidewalks, and cars.

They took thousands of smear samples consisting of anything they could wipe up from a surface using a four-inch-by-four-inch cotton cloth. If so much as one atom of radioactive contamination escaped from the Containment Vessel, the HPs were going to find it, isolate it, isolate the source of it, and clean it up. To say that they were good at what they did would not be giving them near enough credit.

*****

One of the people who went into the remote guard shack after the HP scan was Lenell Spector. The guards at the main gate had taken the folder with her resume in it. *So much for working on my resume*, Lenell thought.

She had stuffed the door-open printouts into her purse. As she walked down the access road, it dawned on her that the bogus entry alarms, the man Brian had seen this morning, and this morning's unprecedented evacuation might all be related. She didn't believe in coincidences.

She walked into the guard shack and announced that she was going to use the computer. The guard on duty nodded and looked back out the front window.

Using her remote login key, she logged into the main plant computers through the telephone switchboard and started typing her request. First, she wanted to compare the printout she had brought down from her office to a newer printout. Then, she wanted to scan the entries for the last hour. She took the printouts (new and old) and sat down at a desk off to one side.

The tenth entry down caught her interest. The time and door were the same, but the name was different. Now, it seemed, a foreign national who quit several weeks ago, went through the door, not a member of the HP staff. A quick scan showed other errant entries. Whoever changed the names in the first place had changed them back and left her a roadmap of incorrect entries and, more importantly, a map of his route through the plant.

Chapter Fifteen

By 8:45 a.m., Brian was busy with the thousand and one little operating tasks associated with shutting down a destroyed nuclear power plant. He was also trying to keep up with a written account of the morning. Jack Smithson walked back into the control room after escorting all the nonessential personnel to the security gate.

Brian walked over to him and said, "I called the power dispatcher and apologized for dumping our electrical production, for becoming such a large electrical load, and for creating so much disturbance on the grid. He wanted to know when we could come back online and could re-assume load. I told him that I didn't speak for management, but that it wouldn't be today. You might want to call him and smooth the situation over some more."

Jack nodded, "I have a lot of calls to make. I'm setting up a command center in the conference room for now."

"Brian, what happened?"

Brian related all the events as best he could remember while he kept one eye on the control consoles.

"I better call the local NRC inspector and break the news. He's going to love this," Jack said with quiet resignation.

Brian took Jack's arm. "We better call an ambulance for Downing. I think he's in shock. I hope he's only in shock."

The two men looked at Downing. He was sitting in the back of the control room watching the goings-on with a bit of a smile on his face. He had the appearance of a doting grandpa sitting on a park bench watching his grandchildren on a swing set.

"Beautiful day, nice weather," Downing muttered over and over to no one in particular.

Jack said, "I'll call," then left for the new command center in the conference room.

Brian turned back to the control console. He would have no trouble finding a crisis to address. Food and drinks appeared in the command center. He also knew that no one was going home any time soon.

*****

At that same moment, Mierie pulled his boat up alongside the dock. He stepped out of the boat and prepared to pull the boat out of the water. His mind was working overtime trying to figure a way to contact Joseph and let him know that Alex James had disappeared. He was more than a little troubled by the turn of events.

*****

At a little past nine, at the remote parking lot guard shack, Lenell stepped to the counter and took the in-house phone from a young woman who was hanging up. She didn't want to try going through the plant switchboard, considering the events of the morning. Without a glance at the exasperated man who was next in line, Lenell dialed the control room.

*****

As Lenell was dialing, Brian was standing in the conference room door.

Christina stepped over to Brian. "Brian, I think I've found something. I need to show you over here," she said as she moved back to the reactor control console. Before she could finish, the control room phone rang. Brian picked it up.

"Control room!" he snapped, harder than he intended. During a Class One Evacuation, no one was supposed to call the control room unless it was a life-or-death situation, and then had better have a good explanation. Somebody had better have a good reason for tying up the phone.

"Control room!" he answered again, with more edge than he intended.

"This is Lenell Spector. This is a plant emergency. Let me talk to Brian Sing. Do it now!" she instructed.

"Lenell, this is Brian. Whatever it is: not now. We're code red busy," he started to hang up. Inside, he was glad she called. Hearing her voice calmed him, centered him. She could talk about anything and bring a unique perspective to him. He would have benefitted from explaining this whole thing to her, but now wasn't the time.

"Brian, listen to me. I think that I've found your thief. He may still be in the plant. I'm on my way to the Personnel Access Center. Get me added to the list of essential personnel. Your thief may be involved with whatever is going on in there. Brian? Brian? Did you hear me?"

"I'll call security right now. Come to the control room." He hung up.

Dax walked into the control room to where Brian was standing.

He waited until Brian acknowledged him.

Brian focused his attention on the senior security guard, a sergeant. "Please add Lenell Spector to the list of essential personnel on my authority. She will arrive at the Personnel Access Center in a few minutes. Have her escorted to the control room."

The sergeant said, "Yes, Sir." He nodded to one of the guards standing next to him.

The guard said, "On my way, Sarge." He marched out of the control room like a soldier reporting for duty.

Brian turned to Dax. "I had to initiate a boron injection to shut down the reactor. I'm certain that we're out of the woods, but I don't want to take any chances. Find an HP chemist, refill, and recharge the Boron Injection System. Come back here when you're done."

"Got it," Dax said as he also turned and left the control room with definite purpose in his step.

For the next few minutes, both Brian and Christina were involved, but not with each other. When she was free, Christina stepped over to Brian again and said, "Brian, I need to show you something. It may be important." Again, she stepped over to the reactor control console.

She pointed to the console as she explained, "One of the steps in my emergency shutdown procedure is to manually open the Primary Coolant Relief Valves. They don't seem to be working properly. When I turn the 'A' relief valve to open, nothing happens. The computer and indicator lights both say that the valve is closed, which is its normal operating position. When I turn the 'B' relief valve to open, both the computer and indicator lights reflect that the valve did, in fact, change to the normal open shut-down position. When I operate the 'C' relief valve, the indicator lights show the valve as closed in normal operating position. The computer inputs say that the 'C' valve is stuck somewhere mid-stroke. That's three different and conflicting sets of indicating data."

Brian processed this latest information, and then thought aloud, "Sounds like the relief valve control cables may have been damaged. Let me think about it for a few minutes. Start a plant work request for the electrical shop to check them out but not to make any corrections until after the incident investigation."

Christina nodded and went to check on the operating status of her diesels.

An announcement came over the PA system in the control room, "The Turbine-Generator Turning Gear is engaged." Christina repeated, "The Turbine-Generator Turning Gear is engaged" and made a log entry. The next hour went by in a blur of log entries, equipment starts, equipment stops, and announcements.

At a few minutes to ten, Lenell walked into the control room with her guard escort. Brian wasn't prepared for the rush of emotions that flooded him when he saw her. He had been concentrating on the power plant and had forgotten that she was coming to talk to him. She was so beautiful and regal. His heart skipped a beat at the sight of her. He knew. At that moment, he knew.

He knew that he would grow and learn from her in all the most positive ways. He hoped there would be some ways that he could be a part of her growth, as well. He took a moment and watched her as she thanked the guard for walking with her to the control room. She smiled at him. The guard fawned.

Lenell looked away from the guard and spotted Brian staring at her. She was curious about the intimacy of the stare. She motioned to a side table and took the computer pages out of her purse. As she walked to the table, she wondered what was going through his mind. She had a feeling that it wasn't the computer pages.

"Good morning, Lenell," he said as he walked over to her. It took some effort to get his focus back to the power plant. What he wanted to do was start quoting sappy song lyrics, but when Lenell spoke in a professional tone, it snapped him back to task. He would think back many times in the future on this sudden, momentary lapse. It was so out of character for him. It was strange. Something else that he would always remember, was that he liked the feeling.

Lenell gave him a brief, courtesy smile and launched into her presentation, "I found your intruder from this morning, Mr. Cargo Vest. Someone has learned to reprogram the door access security computer to make it look like the wrong people are asking for permission to open doors. Some of these people are employees who weren't at Desert Canyons today. Others no longer even work for the utility. I was able to follow Mr. Cargo Vest through the plant. You did follow him to the ground floor of the Turbine Building high bay, but he didn't leave the building. He entered the Penetration Access Hallway and through door PSB-34. He went through that door forty-five seconds after you went through the Maintenance Building exit. A minute later, he opened the door to Cable Penetration Room 24. I suspect that he went inside, but he didn't come back out. I think that he's still in Cable Penetration Room 24. He may have just opened the door and then stepped back into the access hallway. Either way, he didn't exit the hallway. He's either hiding in the hallway or he is still in CPR 24. It also means that he had help in changing the access authorizations while he was moving around." She took a deep breath and looked at him, waiting for a reaction.

"Wow," was all he could say. "That's excellent work. This guy was smart. He went in because he knew I would go out," he added after a short pause. He started to look around the control room for someone to send to investigate Cable Penetration Room

24. As an afterthought, he turned back to Lenell and asked, "Are you busy? Can you work from here today? The conference room is our impromptu command center. I have a feeling we're going to need more of your expertise as the day goes on."

"Sure," she said as she walked away.

*****

As Lenell sat down in the command center, Mierie sat down at his laptop computer in his apartment. He was composing a message for one of the dating bulletin boards explaining that Alex James had disappeared. He didn't know when Josef/Babar might check his dating services, but he was prepared to remove each entry after one day and post a new message on another bulletin board. After he posted his message, he went down to the parking lot, changed the license plates on his car, and left town. As he drove away, he also left the Mierie name behind. He assumed the identity of Gilbert Johnson, independent contractor from New York, on vacation. Gilbert worried himself to distraction all the way to Las Vegas.

*****

For the next couple of hours, operations in the control room were as reserved as they could be considering that the operating staff was recovering from a major nuclear accident. There were dozens of quick, little meetings. An army of off-duty operators had shown up and assigned dozens of small errands. Every few minutes, more HP reports came in declaring another building, space or area was free of contamination. Brian and Jack were beginning to feel as though they at least dodged part of the bullet. The local NRC Inspector for Southern California showed up at 11:00 a.m. Smithson and the NRC representative were looking through notebooks of NRC reporting regulations and requirements.

Dax walked into the control room at a quarter to twelve and announced, "The 'Boron Injection System' is charged and in standby."

"Thanks, Dax. It looks like we may not need it," Brian said with a relaxed smile. "It looks like containment held. What time did you get here this morning?" Brian asked.

"Four," Dax answered. "But I can stay as long as you need me."

"Good. I need you to stay on until around six. We've a lot to do. We had a report of an unauthorized entry to room CPR-24 this morning.

We don't have a report of anyone exiting the room. Check it out. See if anything is out of the ordinary," Brian instructed. Dax left the control room.

Something was needling Brian as he went back to work. He kept thinking, *CPR-24, CPR-24, what was it? Why did CPR-24…!"* Brian had an epiphone. He picked up the PA microphone. "Dax, come back to the control room. Dax, report to the control room, stat." He hung up the mike.

"Christina, did you start that relief valve work request, yet?" he asked.

"No, sorry, I haven't. I've had too many other things to do. I'll get right on it," she answered with a little bit of apology in her voice.

"Table it, for now. Find out where the cables for relief valves A and C enter the Containment Vessel. Do it now, highest priority. Interrupt me when you know."

Dax walked back into the control room. Brian motioned him over to where the security guards huddled in an animated discussion. As the small group assembled, Brian said to the security officer in charge, "We had a report that an unknown person that we called Mr. Cargo Vest might be stealing hardware from the high bay shelves. We have a computer report that an unknown person entered a containment penetration room this morning. There was no computer report of him leaving that room. That person's presence in containment penetration CPR-24 may be related to the incident this morning."

Christina put up a hand from across the control room. "CPR-24," she shouted.

"That person seemed to enter, but not leave CPR-24," he continued. "The three primary coolant relief valves have been found to be operating …erratically. The control cables for the relief vales enter containment through CPR-24. I want Dax to check it. I don't know if this person is involved or not. I don't know if he's in there, and I don't know if he's dangerous. Send a couple of guards with Dax. I don't know what, if anything, to expect. Dax, take an HP with you, as well. Background radiation will be highest at the containment wall. I do not want you getting an overdose."

The security OIC said, "I'll go myself. Peters, you're with me. Lead the way, Mr. Dax."

"It's just Dax. They're my initials. This way," he said and led the way out of the control room.

"Christina, I'm expecting a call from Dax on the control room extension in a few minutes. I'll take it in the conference room. When the call comes in, please join us," he said to Christina, not expecting an answer.

He walked into the conference room and said, "Jack, Lenell, please stay. Everyone else, give us this room."

When the three of them were alone, Brian explained the coincidence to Jack and told him that it was Lenell who first spotted the inconsistencies. Then, they waited for several long minutes for Dax to call.

When the Control Room phone rang, Christina answered it and held the receiver toward Brian. When he picked up, she hung up and joined them in the conference room.

Brian put the phone on speaker and asked, "What did you find?"

Dax answered in a calm voice, "The room is pristine. There is no damage that I can see. Nothing seems to be out of place."

Chapter Sixteen

"Well, that is, except for the dead man lying face down in the middle of the floor," he said in a mock deadpan voice. "He's been here for a while. He's cool to the touch. I don't see any injuries; there are no wounds or blood. He looks like he fell asleep. He's wearing a green cargo vest and pants, and has a temporary employee ID with the name Alex James. Brian, the background radiation is high in here. We're against the containment wall. What do you want us to do?"

"Take the body out to the turbine high bay. Search him. Call me back. Ask the security sergeant to return to the control room as soon as possible."

Brian looked at Jack. Jack looked at Brian. "This was no accident," they said in unison.

Lenell asked, "Was this sabotage?"

Christina looked into the control room. "Are we sure he was working alone?" She remembered how oddly Dense David was acting. No, she was certain that David was just being David.

"Christina, double-check every alarm and indicator that comes up. Don't trust any single piece of information. Verify all indicators. Assume that someone is still working against us and expect more trouble. Also, call the floor operators to come to the control room. Fill them in. From now on, no one goes anywhere alone. Bring anyone found alone inside the security fence to the control room. Pass the word face-to-face. Nothing gets broadcast on the PA or phone systems."

Jack said, "I've got to call this in to downtown. This incident just became an FBI matter. I'll ask management to call the state police and request some supplemental support to the security staff." Jack turned and sat down at one of the phones in the conference room without waiting for an answer. He picked up the phone, and dialed the vice president of operations' offices downtown. This was going to be a difficult phone call.

Brian stepped into the control room and scanned the operating consoles. Nothing had changed in the last few minutes, but everything had seemed to change. HPs brought in updated contamination profiles. Operators updated the Control Room Operating Logbook. Security guards watched everything with an air of boredom. Brian forced himself to make a slow, deliberate assessment. Everything seemed as it should be.

Lenell stepped up beside Brian. "Brian, Dax is on the phone."

He stepped back into the conference room and put the phone on speaker. "Dax, did you search the body?"

"Not yet," Dax replied.

"Do it now. I want to know everything that's in his pockets."

"Okay. You know about the temporary security badge on the outside of his vest pocket. Oh ho, this is interesting. There are four more Desert Canyon badges in his vest pocket: Harold Robert, Bayani Bangit…"

Lenell interrupted Dax, "Sharron Nelson and Jan Isben."

"That's right."

"Those were the four names used for bogus entries. Bayani left the utility and returned to the Philippines. Nelson quit and moved out of state with her husband. Harold reported his badge missing at work. Jan lost hers at the health club."

Brian nodded and asked, "Anything else?"

"I have one plant security do-not-copy key–number CCH-127, a tube of instant epoxy, and a business card-sized piece of paper with what looks like a Desert Canyons phone number on it. In his pants pockets there are a 5/8 and a 3/4-inch wrench, some small electronics tools, and a small handful of trash left over from some wiring work. I have a key ring with two keys, possibly an apartment key and a Ford car key. I have a brand-new wallet with a few dollars, and a California driver's license issued to one Alex James. There's no other form of ID."

"Dax, Bring everything from his pockets to the control room. Ask the guards with you to please stay with the body until the ambulance gets here."

"Will do," Dax answered.

Brian turned to Lenell, "Will you monitor the access request entries as they come in? If someone here was working with Mr. Cargo Vest, he may still try to move around the plant."

Lenell nodded.

Brian stepped into the control room and said to Christina, "Christina, call the downtown key control office and find out what lock key CCH-127 fits. Also, ask for a list of everyone who has a copy of that key. Maybe the accomplice is on that list."

Brian scanned the control room. Something was nagging at him in the back of his mind. He looked back into the conference room. Jack was on one of the lines. There were several others set up on the main conference room. Buffet cold cuts were on a portable table in the back. He looked at his watch. It was 12:40 p.m., lunchtime. There was food, but he wasn't hungry. *There are several phones,* he thought. *What am I missing?* He had been busy with a dozen details a minute for most of the morning. Who could guess how many critical things he had overlooked?

The piece of paper with a number on it crept back to the front of his mind. *It might be the office phone of Mr. Cargo Vest's accomplice or it could be the trigger for a remote bomb.* He'd already thought of those possibilities. The last thing that they needed was an explosion on top of everything else. A hydrogen explosion! He hadn't addressed the possibility of a hydrogen build up in containment. Hydrogen had been building up at an unknown rate for five and a half hours.

He closed his eyes in exasperation at his oversight. A hydrogen explosion at this time wouldn't destroy the Containment Vessel; Engineers designed it to survive an internal explosion of that magnitude, but an explosion of any kind might blow the seals on some of the penetrations. With the post-accident pressure in containment, losing even one seal would mean losing a lot of contaminated sludge out of the Containment Vessel and into the surrounding building.

Jack was between calls. Brian asked, "Jack, who is the duty HP?"

"Nathan Clark," Jack answered, then went back to his calls.

Brian called Nathan Clark. Brian guessed that it was a waste of time because Clark should be in the plant with his radiation survey teams, but he had to try.

"Clark," Clark answered.

"Nathan, Brian Sing here. Can you come to the control room for a few minutes?"

"Not now, Brian, maybe at four?"

"Let me rephrase my request. Come to the control room."

"I'll be there in five."

"It's important, thanks," Brian said more softly. The skill of giving direct orders that left no room for compromise had left him when he separated from the Army. He was surprised at how easily he had fallen back into his role of Army officer.

Three minutes later, Nathan Clark walked into the control room and gestured to Brian.

Brian walked over to Nathan and gave a glance back into the control room. "Nathan, I think that we may have a genuine problem on our hands. Remember last year, when we found a small quantity of unknown radioactive waste in a non-radioactive reserve waste tank? We had meetings for weeks debating the controversy, 'we can't open the vent to test the gasses because we don't know what's in the tank' and 'we don't know what's in the tank because we can't open the vent?'"

"I remember that we talked a non-problem to death for six months."

"You know we had a fuel breach this morning. I'm concerned that hydrogen has been building up in containment all morning."

"That isn't good," Nathan said. "You know that I have no power of approval to vent containment during an accident."

"If I make a Deviation of Operation Standards request, management will book a conference room."

"What do I need to do?"

"I can request a limited, non-standard sampling program without management approval, right?"

Nathan nodded.

"Take a series of xenon concentration samples from the containment high point vent. Can you do that on the down low?"

"How big a sample?" Nathan took on a conspiratorial tone.

"How big a sample can you take at one time?"

"A liter."

"I am placing a verbal work order for a one-liter xenon concentration sample from the high point vent. How long does it take to draw a one-liter sample?"

"About ten minutes."

"I want a sample every fifteen minutes. Analyze for the percent by weight of xenon and the percent by weight of hydrogen in every sample. Use standard vented waste disposal protocols for the remains of each sample. Report the results every four hours. Consider it routine, low key."

Nathan looked at Brian and said, "I hope you know what you're doing," and then left the control room.

Chapter Seventeen

As Nathan left the control room, he mentally calculated how many HPs it was going to take to execute Brian's xenon monitoring request. The room around the high point vent was a high radiation zone. No one HP could enter the room twice in a twenty-four-hour period. Nathan passed the security sergeant entering the control room.

"I understand that this is now an Incident Command Center. For the time being, plant security will work from here as well. I am now the Crisis Officer in Charge. We have an unexplained dead body. This is beyond my authority and jurisdiction," he said to Brian.

"Jack is calling the state police to provide support for your staff to set up a perimeter. He's also calling the FBI to take custody of the body and the sabotage investigation. I've asked that everyone observe the buddy system for the time being. Nobody works alone or goes anywhere alone."

"Good idea. Was this sabotage?"

Brian nodded silently.

The OIC said, "I've ordered that all security personnel be issued weapons while on duty inside the perimeter fence until we find out if we're in any danger, here. Do you want a weapon?"

Brian thought about the offer, but said, "No need. I trust your men to keep us safe. But I do need you to assign a man to escort Dax whenever he leaves the control room."

The OIC motioned to a guard nearby who was now carrying an efficient-looking, black, automatic rifle. "Who is Dax?"

As if on cue, Dax walked into the control room carrying a plastic supermarket bag.

"That's Dax."

The OIC said to his guard, "This is Dax. You're his escort whenever he leaves the control room until I say otherwise. Nothing will happen to him, correct?" It was an order, not a question.

Dax raised and eyebrow at Brian, "Escort?"

"We are observing the buddy system until we're sure this thing is over. Let's see what you've got."

Dax laid out the items from Mr. Cargo Vest's pockets.

Lenell picked up one of the badges, "Brian, these are real." *Lucy, somebody has some 'splaining to do,* she pantomimed under her breath. "These were the only four IDs invol- ved in the bogus entries that I found. I don't think that anyone else is still on site. If they are, they're not going through any doors."

Brian nodded.

From her place at the control console, Christina turned around and said, "Brian, key CCH-127 is for Containment Sump Blow-Down Valve 127. No new key issues for the last six months. If that valve had ope- ned, half the sludge in containment would have ended up at the River Water Pump House."

Dax spoke up, "I was at the pump house this morning when this happened. I was discharging the di- lute waste tank into the river."

"Mr. Cargo Vest used one of his badges to enter the River Water Pump House the night you saw him outside the Maintenance Building," Lenell added.

Jack said, "Son, I think you might have dodged a bullet this mor- ning." Jack obviously didn't know about the 45 automatic hidden in the desert. "I'm going to call this number and see who was playing footsy with our man here."

"No!" ordered Brian. "It may not be a person. This trash is from an electric installation of some sort. We don't know what the call might trigger. Dax, contact someone from plant communications. Don't let them call the number. Ask if they have a record of who the number is assigned to. I'll bet we find that it isn't. If it's not assigned, ask if they can ping the number and tell us its location without making it ring. I also want to know if they can disable the number. Make the computer play a message about being out of service if anyone calls. If we can do all that, ask if we can trace the caller ID of all calls to that number from now on. Got all that?"

Dax thought for a second, smiled, then turned to the phones to make the call.

Lenell said to Brian almost as an aside, "I sure would like to know what killed Mr. Cargo Vest."

"You mean Mr. Alex James?"

"I don't think his real name is Alex James. Besides, Mr. Cargo Vest fits him better." She smiled.

Brian panned his attention around to the control room door in time to see one of the armed security personnel enter the control room with two paramedics toting a gurney.

Brian went back to examining the operator's consoles.

Christina led the paramedics over to Downing.

"Beautiful day, nice weather," Downing said.

As they started their evaluation, Brian was glad that Christina had intercepted the paramedics. For Brian, the morning had been one crisis after another. He wanted to take a few minutes and check out *his* power plant. He wanted to know how damaged she was. He lost himself in the analysis of the various meters and gauges. His focus melted into a mosaic of computer readouts and log entries.

After a minute or two, Jack walked over and told the paramedics about the dead body in the turbine high bay and that the FBI was on the way. At 1:30 p.m., as the paramedics were getting ready to ask Jack about the body, four men in business suits entered the control room. The FBI had arrived.

The lead agent addressed Brian, "Good Afternoon. My name is Special Agent in Charge Michael Corazal, FBI." All four showed their credentials. "Can you tell me who's in charge here?"

Before Brian could speak, Jack stepped up and introduced himself, "I'm Jack Smithson, Plant Manager for Desert Canyons. This is Brian Sing, Operations Shift Supervisor. If it has to do with the power plant operation and safety, Mr. Sing makes all the decisions. If it's a management question, I'm the man. I don't see our Security OIC right now. He must have stepped out."

"I met your Security OIC at the entrance when we got our visitors' badges."

"Step into our impromptu command center so we don't interfere with the operating staff. I'll tell you what I know."

Two of the agents followed Jack into the command center. Brian noticed one of the remaining agents was setting up a video camera, and the other had taken out a pad and pencil and was taking notes.

He tried to ignore them and go back to his plant.

Christina spoke, "Brian, first reports on the xenon sampling are in: xenon levels are below regulation levels, hydrogen concentrations are elevated."

Brian nodded.

Dax stepped up, "Brian, the phone number's not assigned. The tech pinged it. It's active. It's connected to a jack in CPR-24, the room where we found Mr. Cargo Vest. The technician disabled the number. If anyone calls, they'll get a recording that the number isn't in service. The phone won't ring. As far as a trace goes, if the call originates inside the electronic firewall, we can lock the source. If the call originates outside the plant switchboard, the local phone company will have to trace it."

"Come with me. Christina, you have the control room."

"I have the control room." *Such as it is,* she thought.

Brian and Dax walked into the command center. Brian said, "Gentlemen, excuse me for interrupting. We have an operations situation."

Jack stopped mid-sentence. SAIC Corazal turned his attention to Brian with genuine interest. The stereotype of the FBI agent wearing sunglasses and earpieces was a television creation, same as the one of American Indians riding horses in a circle around a wagon train like ducks in a sideshow shooting gallery. The FBI did not rudely take over the investigation. They didn't insult and trivialize the local yokels with pithy comebacks. They were on site to help and lend assistance. SAIC Corazal prided himself in the fact that his men were team players. If the operations supervisor thought that something was important enough to interrupt the ongoing conversations in the room, Corazal knew that he should shut up and listen.

Brian continued, "We found the body of Alex James in an access-controlled room called CPR-24. In his pocket was a piece of paper with a phone number on it. We have information that that number was active in room CPR-24. Mr. James had a small handful of electrical wiring debris in his pockets. Priority one, we need to investigate that connection. Would you agree, Special Agent In Charge Corazal?"

Corazal said, "Call me Michael. And I couldn't agree more."

"Dax, take your escort and an HP and check out that connection. Tell the HP not to let anyone get burned up, (receive a dose of radiation exceeding the daily plant limit)."

Agent Corazal added, "One of my men go along. We don't know what we're facing quite yet." He turned to his agent and asked, "You have your camera? I want a lot of art (pictures)."

Brian nodded and added, with an attempt at levity, "Dax, don't let the fed get burned up, either."

After the group left, Agent Corazal continued to listen to Jack's account of the morning. When Jack finished, he turned attention to the contents of Mr. Cargo Vest's pockets. After a minute, he said, "I agree. You may have a bigger problem. Be ready for it. I need to talk to the paramedics."

Michael stepped over to the paramedics and said, "My name is Special Agent In Charge Michael Corazal. What are your names?"

"We're Harden McMasters and Steven Wells. I'm pleased to meet you."

"How's Mr. Downing? Is he stable?"

"Beautiful day, nice weather," Downing said again.

"He's stable, but I think he may have had a small stroke. He doesn't seem to be able to form short-term memories. That's why he keeps repeating himself. He remembers that he wants to say something, but he can't remember having said it."

"I'd like one of you to stay with him. I'd like the other to come with me to examine the corpse. When you transport, you will take Mr. James's body to the FBI morgue in Los Angeles. An FBI medical team will perform the autopsy on Mr. James. We also want one of our doctors to examine Mr. James. Then you'll be free to bring Mr. Downing back to a local hospital for treatment. The trip to LA is considered sensitive information. There may be Homeland Security issues. Please, don't release the information to anyone."

Both nodded.

Brian absently noticed the SAIC and paramedic leave the control room with Jack. He was making a log entry, "1:45 p.m., Containment Recirculation Filters High Differential. Containment Recirculation Fans secured." He thought, *what is plugging the filters?*

*****

At the same moment, Mierie/ Gilbert was entering the outskirts of Las Vegas. He was looking for something amongst the businesses along the highway, and he found it. It was a nondescript, aging diner next to a gas station. In the parking lot between them was a glass phone booth. He stopped, stepped into the booth, and wrote down the number. When he got back into his car, he reset his odometer to zero and continued his drive into Las Vegas.

He also stopped at a convenience store and bought two burner phones. He would use each once and then conceal the phone on an outbound eighteen-wheeler at a random truck stop. Let the authorities chase it all over the countryside if they wanted to.

*****

It was 3:45 in LaPlace, Louisiana. Josef/Babar was sitting down to watch the early news on a television station from California. The nuclear power plant, scheduled for a refueling shutdown today, *shut itself down.* Management ordered all unnecessary staff evacuated and sent home indefinitely. We're told that the incident was minor and that the utility will release more information as it becomes available. Some people will do anything for a day off." The newscaster turned to the cohost, "John?"

Wait… what?… wait, that was it? That's the whole report? Babar/Josef shouted to himself. *The incident was minor? Someone wanted a day off.* Babar/Josef rushed to his computer and began scanning the social web sites.

*****

Twenty minutes later, Agent Corazal and the paramedic returned. The paramedics took Downing out on a gurney.

"Beautiful day, nice weather," Downing seemed pleased with himself.

Lenell wondered if it was going to be *a beautiful day and nice weather* for the rest of his life.

At 4:55 p.m., California time, the operations swing shift arrived at the Desert Canyons control room ready to take over operations. Jack waved them into the command center.

Jack stepped up next to Brian, "Brian, management would like you to stay in charge of operations for the time being, if you agree. That means day shift from seven to five until we decide otherwise. You'll be the man. Other personnel will cover the back shifts under your instructions. You can have whatever staff you want on days."

"I want Christina in the control room. I want Downing's and my floor operators. Dax will be my personal assistant. I think that we should ask Lenell to set up a document control library."

Like most everyone else at Desert Canyons, the utility no longer needed her services.

"We can have the HPs clear the big conference room and bring in some file cabinets. It's going to be a huge paper project."

"Done."

"Brief the oncoming shift and let them take over. Stay around until five in case there are any questions. Get some good sleep tonight. Tomorrow may be an even worse day than today. Good?"

Before Jack and Brian could go back into the command center, Dax and crew returned from their investigation of the phone line in CPR-24.

Dax started to speak.

Brian said, "Wait. I want the oncoming shift to hear this."

When everyone had settled down, Brian briefed the oncoming shift. Then, he looked at Dax.

Dax said, "There was a cable connected to the phone jack in CPR-24. Whoever installed the cable did a thorough job hiding it in the cable trays. Our suspect terminated the cable in a small, homemade aluminum box. The box's internal electronics were integrated into the wiring for the primary coolant relief valve control circuits up against the penetration. We have pictures."

The agent passed his camera around. Brian recognized the box as the one he saw Mr. Cargo Vest remove from the high bay that morning.

"The box is fourteen inches by five inches by four inches. We feel that, as large and as heavy as it is, it must contain more than circuitry. We didn't touch it or the connecting cable."

The SAIC said, "With your permission, I can have an FBI bomb squad here in an hour to clear the device." He looked at Brian.

Brian nodded, "Yes, of course. You might bring several bomb crews. As non-permanent staff, your stay time in that room with its high radiation background is twenty minutes a day. I don't want to burn (overexpose) any of your people."

"Thank you. We'll investigate the box and, if necessary, defuse it. If there's an explosive, we'll remove it."

Brian said, "Sounds good. I propose we meet here at seven every morning and at four every evening to update everyone on our progress and discuss our next steps. Any news on what killed Alex James?"

Agent Corazal shook his head.

Brian finished the turnover briefing and asked if there were any questions.

"Okay, go to work."

Brian turned to the four floor operators who had been there all day. "The four of you are on permanent days, 7 to 5, until further notice. Any problems? Christina, you're on permanent days, also. Dax, you're my free-lancer, same arrangement, okay? If you need time off, see me. We're going to get a lot of overtime. Go home, all of you, and get some sleep. We'll see you at seven."

After another hour, Jack and Brian left the plant. Both were too tired to drive, which was okay since they couldn't get their vehicles out of the parking lot, anyway. A security guard drove them to their homes and made arrangements to pick them up in the morning. For them, the day was over.

*****

As the car pulled up in front of Brian's residence, Josef/Babar picked up the receiver from a public phone. He dialed the number for the incendiary box and listened to the message that the number was no longer in service.

At least one thing went right, he thought. *The incendiary box must have destroyed itself.* For Josef/Babar, the day was over as well.

Chapter Eighteen

On May 2nd at 6:00 a.m. in LaPlace, Louisiana, (4:00 a.m. in Las Vegas and Los Angeles); Josef/Babar found the notice from Mierie on the dating service. The coded posting asked for an 8:07 a.m. landline call to a coded number in Las Vegas. That translated to 10:07 a.m. LaPlace time, four hours from then. Four hours might well have been four months. Josef/Babar decoded the phone number and put it in his pocket.

*****

At 6:30 a.m. Los Angeles time, an unmarked California State Police car arrived at Brian's door.

On the drive in, Brian asked, "Any updates from last night?"

"Sorry, our contract is for outside security." He paused and looked over at Brian, who was frowning, "But there wasn't any noticeable activity last night, if that helps."

"Thanks."

The rest of the ride was quiet.

When Brian got out of the car at the Desert Canyons remote parking lot, Jack was waiting for him. They rode the rest of the way to the main plant in a security vehicle.

"Anything new?"

"I haven't heard a thing, which is good news."

They walked through the main control room and into the command center. Operations and security people trickled in. Dense David was there with his new crew. They were just going off shift. Management never discovered his involvement. Christina came in after Brian. Agent Corazal was already there.

"Good news," Michael said with a nod.

When everyone had a pastry and coffee and had settled down, Jack opened, "Good morning, everybody. Settle down and we'll start. Agent Corazal," Jack passed the baton to Michael.

"Good morning," Agent Corazal said. "Everyone knows the story up until five last night, correct?"

Many nodded, but no one answered.

"Members of the FBI Bomb Squad opened and examined the device in CPR-24 overnight. The box was supposed to be the trigger for a two-pound block of C-4. It also acted to subvert the operation of several relays in the control wiring circuits for the Primary Coolant Relief Valves."

Turning to an aide, he asked, "Do we have some of the pictures?"

As the aide circulated printed copies of the trigger box from several different perspectives, Agent Corazal returned his focus to the assembled group, "We speculate that the device is designed to interrupt the normal operations of the relief valves and then incinerate itself and most of the cable tray hardware around it. We have removed the incendiary material and unplugged the box from the jack. We seeded a rumor that there was a small fire in a remote corner of the plant."

"At 5:24 p.m. last night, a call was received from outside the plant telecommunications system firewall for the number coded into the device. The call didn't go through. The phone company was able to trace the call to St. John's Parish in Louisiana. The caller didn't stay on long enough for them to nail down a more detailed location."

"Mr. Sing, Mr. Smithson, we would like to examine the device at our forensics lab in L.A. Will you have some of your electrical techs remove it for us at your earliest convenience?"

Jack said, "Of course." Brian looked at Dax, who got up and left the room.

"We found Mr. James's car and moved it inside the maintenance bay. We believe that there are no other conspirators at large inside the plant security perimeter. We'll terminate the buddy system protocol later this afternoon. That's all the information that I can release about our investigation at this point. Agents will be coming around to each of you throughout the day, verifying and refining your statements. Please give them your full cooperation. Mr. Sing, we will interview your operating staff while they work. Mr. Smithson."

Jack said, "Okay, let's go through a full shift change briefing. Everybody, be safe." With that, the various operators paired off with their counterparts and began to share information.

Brian and the outgoing Operations Shift Supervisor, Thomas Kayne, walked into the control room. Dax was still on the phone. Brian caught Dax's attention, "I want those control circuits restored once the box is out. I want everything to be working as close to normal as possible so we can be more certain what equipment might still be malfunctioning."

Dax nodded and went back to his call.

Within minutes, a small army of electrical and instrument technicians and a dozen HPs descended on the access point outside of CPR-24. Engineers produced drawings showing circuit design, wire connection details, and cable tray layout. A stack of pertinent photos of the room appeared. As soon as the door opened, a stream of technicians carried lead bricks into the room and stacked them against the Containment Vessel wall. The bricks reduced the amount of background radiation that was pouring into the room. The more the HPs could reduce the radiation levels, the longer the techs could work in the room.

Technicians installed a maze of small ladders and platforms. Everyone wore a safety harness. Everyone seemed to accept that he or she might be working in this room for a long while. Every touchable surface was swabbed with a clean cotton cloth, which was electronically scanned for spreadable contamination. Recirculating fans with high-efficiency filters were set up to guarantee that the air was NASA "clean room" clean.

When the electrical techs had convinced themselves that they knew all there was to know about the job at hand, and that they could do it with their eyes closed, they stepped in. The first pair of techs took their positions and disconnected power leads. After fifteen minutes, the first pair of techs left the room, and a second pair took their place. The whole team worked with surgical precision. HPs monitored everything. The job would take twenty-four hours.

Elsewhere in the plant, Dax watched a crew set up lead bricks around the Containment Recirculating Air Filter Housing, which was heavily contaminated and emitting a serious radiation hazard. When the shielding was in place, HPs used a remote-controlled robot to remove the filter cartridges and put them into a heavily shielded radioactive waste shipping container. HPs used the robot to install new filter canisters and then restarted the fans. In a couple of hours, the process would be repeated, and continue to be repeated ten to fourteen times a day until they could operate the fans without the filters becoming contaminated. Trucks arrived at the remote parking lot security blockade to transport the radioactive waste shipping containers to a radioactive waste disposal facility, like the one at Hanford in Washington State.

Elsewhere in the plant, the floor operators lined up the pumps and valves needed to draw water from the containment sump and pass it through chemical treatment equipment designed to cause dissolved minerals to turn back into solid minerals. Filters would then catch the solidified minerals. HPs processed the solid mineral filters the same way as the airborne filters. When the water was clean to the specifications in the procedure, it was pumped back to the fire-suppression manifold that circled the containment ceiling. The processed water was, once again, washed down over everything that was in containment, collecting new, dissolvable solids. Operators would repeat the filtering every few hours for months, maybe years. They would ship tons of waste, on hundreds of trucks, documenting every container. The HPs added chemical solvents to the wastewater when repeated cleaning cycles did not collect significant amounts of contaminated solids. And the washing process would start again.

Elsewhere in the plant, a team of mechanics was building a huge, submarine-type double-door hatch to be attached to the main containment hatch. The doors interlocked to prevent both of them from opening at the same time, therefore no unplanned air (and no contamination) could leak from inside the Containment Vessel. Operators kept the Containment Vessel at a vacuum in the event that the interlocks failed and both doors opened at the same time. When the levels of spreadable contamination in the Containment Vessel were reduced to the lowest possible levels, the containment hatch would open.

Once technicians opened the hatch, they would move lead bricks into containment and stack them around any contaminated equipment. Others would wipe down every available surface. The rags would be added to the contaminated waste shipments. Contaminated surfaces would be re-wiped until nothing more would come off. The surfaces would then be coated with a thousand-year epoxy to further seal them.

Mechanics disassembled the larger pieces of equipment in the Containment Vessel and shipped the parts with the contaminated waste. After they completed decontamination, the Containment Vessel would then be an empty radioactive shell with a thick, epoxy coating. The HP Supervisor and the local NRC representative would then decide how best to further process the containment shell.

The cleanup was slated to be Brain's world for the foreseeable future. The mountain of documents surrounding this cleanup was slated to be Lenell's world for the near future.

It took almost an hour (from 4 to 5 p.m.) for Brian to brief the new shift. At 5:00 p.m., on the first day of the recovery process, an exhausted Brian Sing and his equally-exhausted crew went home. At Desert Canyons, the work continued.

*****

At 6:07 p.m., California time, 8:07 p.m., Louisiana time, Josef/Babar stepped into a phone booth in the French Quarter (the *Vieux Carre'*) in New Orleans.

Mierie/Gilbert answered on the first ring, "Praise be to Allah."

"You are well?" Josef/Babar asked.

"I'm well. And you, Agha?"

"I'm well. You are now Gilbert Johnson, I trust?" Babar/Josef
asked.

"I am," Gilbert answered.
"And how shall I address you?"

"I am Babar Collins," Babar
answered. "Tell me of our last family
reunion?"

"Things went well. Not as
complete as we expected, but well. Of
course, no plan is ever executed perfectly. I heard an evacuation announced over the PA. The reactor must
have been damaged. People were rushing around. Two employees left the
River Water Pump House alive after
the alarms were raised. Alex James
never appeared on the observation
deck. I have received no word from
him."

"I saw no sign that Alex was
physically injured. I do have information that two Desert Canyon employees were hospitalized. I confirmed
that two people, neither of which was
Alex, were indeed hospitalized. No
one seems to be searching for Alex.
His landlady tells me that no one has
been there looking for him. I don't
know if his car is in the parking lot or
not."

"Local news says that there
was a fire in a building that caused

some damage and that the plant will shut down for a while. I have seen no indication that the authorities are searching for anyone. We may be in the clear. We didn't accomplish all our goals, but clearly there was some success. I believe that the divine hand of Allah provided the success that we had and that He smiles on our efforts."

Babar said, "I agree with your analysis. I don't like that Alex has disappeared. Maybe the coward panicked and ran." After a moment he added, "Gilbert, for the next four to six weeks, stay on the move. Stay no more than a couple of days in any one place. Rotate your IDs. Monitor your information sources. I want to be sure that no one is searching for us. Contact me at the end of June. I'll see you then, my friend. Allah be with you."

"Allah be with you as well, Babar." Gilbert hung up and returned to Las Vegas.

Babar returned to his room as well. *Maybe I'll tour The Old South for the next few weeks; Alabama, Florida, Georgia,* Babar thought as he fell asleep.

Chapter Nineteen

Mid-morning the next day, Dax called the control room to let Brian know that the device had been removed from the plant control circuitry. Brian told Dax to release the device to the FBI and to ask the instrument techs how long it would take to restore the circuits.

Lenell was in the conference room with the FBI computer forensics crew monitoring the 'door open' codes. One of the floor operators circulated around the plant, opening and closing doors so the forensics team could watch the lines of code execute.

Jack Smithson sat next to Agent Corazal as he conducted yet another employee interview.

A security guard came into the control room and asked Lenell, Brian, and Jack for their car keys and the makes and models of their cars. Security was having the cars of the operating staff brought to the remote parking lot. HPs would survey each car for radioactive contamination and, if clean, release it to the owner. The FBI would also be conducting a forensic search of the cars. They weren't expecting to find anything, but a little *due diligence* couldn't hurt.

Throughout the day, security personnel escorted individual staff members into the plant to retrieve personal items left in workspaces during the evacuation. Everyone left the plant through the main security checkpoint to retrieve hats, coats, and packages. As they passed the parking lot, each employee retrieved his or her car. After each employee accumulated all their personal belongings, HPs meticulously surveyed each piece for spreadable contamination. The FBI watched. The FBI took new statements. Eventually, the FBI released all the employees.

The FBI compared the new statements to the original statements and to all future statements. For employees with nothing to hide, the statements would be consistent. FBI investigators were looking for inconsistencies. They were convinced that Alex James had an accomplice, and that he was hiding amongst the legitimate employees. If someone had something to hide, inconsistencies in their statements would give them away.

By close of business that evening, the FBI was certain that Mr. Cargo Vest acted alone inside the plant. They removed the requirement for the buddy system. Utility management, however, insisted that security staff remain armed until further notice.

The cleanup, the interviews, and the investigation continued, without incident, for the next ten days. Work life returned to a new normal.

On May 13th, Jack Smithson, Agent Corazal, and the NRC senior investigator entered the control room and asked Brian to step into the conference room.

Agent Corazal spoke first, "Brian, we've been turning in daily reports to our counterparts in D.C. Considering your direct involvement during and after the incident, your name has been mentioned throughout. Seems the president has been reading the briefing materials in some detail and with considerable interest."

"He has asked if the four of us will attend a cabinet-level briefing on the events surrounding the Desert Canyons incident. The four of us will be giving the briefing and answer any questions. Your contribution will focus on what vulnerabilities allowed the attack and what actions might we take to prevent future attacks"

Agent Corazal paused, waited, raised his eyebrows, and paused again.

Brian felt his jaw drop, but just imperceptibly enough that the others didn't notice. He calmly said, "Oh, yes, of course, when?"

Agent Corazal said, "Good. We leave this afternoon."

Jack said, "Your replacement is here. Go home, pack. A car will pick you up a six this evening. We'll be flying one of the FBI's executive jets. If you forget anything, we'll buy new in D.C. Thanks, Brian. Go home."

Brian did. Half an hour later, the other three went home as well.

The cleanup at Desert Canyons continued.

Chapter Twenty

On May 15th, a little over two weeks after the incident at Desert Canyons, Agent Corazal called a noon meeting. The FBI provided a lunch of fruit, cold cuts, and assorted breads. Coffee and soft drinks were also available. All local employees who knew the real facts surrounding the events at Desert Canyons were invited. A much different meeting was being held at the utility's downtown office.

People trickled in for a half an hour. Downing was there: recovered now, but with no memory of the day. He was sporting a visitor's badge and was escorted in by a member of the security force. The two EMTs who took Downing to the hospital and Alex James to the FBI morgue were there. Dax came in with Christina Belvoir, both in good spirits. Brian walked in with Lenell. Miscellaneous other personnel were also present. Selected members of the local police, state police and the FBI filled the open spaces around the outside of the main group. Everyone was jovial, talking in small groups, and enjoying a free lunch.

As soon as most of the people had settled down, Agent Corazal stepped up to the microphone at the head of the table. "I'm Special Agent In Charge Michael Corazal. Everyone present knows me, by now. Anybody here who doesn't know me?" he said, almost joking. He had been in everybody's face for two weeks now. Everybody knew him.

"If everyone pretty well knows everyone else, I'm going to dispense with the round of introductions." He looked around the room. No one moved, so he continued.

"This will be the last formal meeting called by the FBI. We will be leaving the site today. The investigation may go on for months with some of you being interviewed again. I'll post some phone numbers, including mine, for future use. Anyone with a question, comment, or information can call us any time. Today, I'm going to present a picture of what we know about the events of May 1st at Desert Canyons. I'm also going to define our official public statement," he said.

If Brian had heard a statement like that in the past, he would have rolled his eyes, but today, he was beginning to understand the hard reality of intelligence work. Withheld information was a game advantage.

Agent Corazal continued, "I want to remind everyone that, even though we will tell the public that the event is *over*, this is still an open, ongoing investigation," he said with practiced authority as he engaged as many as possible with his direct gaze.

"Today, I'm going to be releasing more information to this group than I would in a normal investigation. FBI procedure says that the FBI will withhold selected critical information from the public. Anyone showing knowledge of withheld information has implicated himself or herself as a person of interest."

"Our situation at Desert Canyons is unique. We have so few substantial leads that we've decided to involve each of you in the investigation. I'm going to give you more information than is in the official press release. I'm going to tell you everything that we can confirm or suspect to-date. I'll withhold nothing."

"What I want each of you to do is to listen to my presentation, take a printed copy of the presentation and commit as much of it to memory as you can. Tell the story we give you here today to anyone who will listen. Listen to anyone who wants to talk about the incident. I want you to listen for discrepancies. If anyone has any information that we haven't included here today, we want to meet them. They may have a source of information that we haven't identified. Without complete and accurate information, you can't do this for us."

"This group is not a bunch of semi-unreliable, street-corner witnesses. You're all professionals of one agency or another. Use all your skills. No discrepancy is too small to report. Does everyone understand what I'm asking you to do?"

Agent Corazal nodded his head in the affirmative to see how many others in the room would mimic his agreement. Most did. Agent Corazal made a mental note of those that he noticed who didn't nod in the affirmative. A couple of the FBI psychologists standing against the outside wall also watched for interesting individual reactions.

"Everyone here has direct knowledge that the event on May 1st wasn't a minor accident. Management is currently holding a meeting downtown for those who don't know it was anything other than a *minor* event. Any questions before I go on?"

Agent Corazal took a moment and put on a show of becoming more relaxed. Again, most of those present seemed to follow his example and made themselves more comfortable, as well. Most of the group was buying in to the request. As before, FBI eyes watched every movement, gesture, and change of expression.

"Okay, first things first. We are certain, let me repeat, certain, that Alex James did not, NOT, act alone. Evidence indicates that he had at least two unknown accomplices. The person who called himself Alex James died of a massive heart attack. His heart had a defect and disintegrated from stress. He died instantly. We have narrowed the identity of Mr. James down to one of three people. We believe that he is most likely an individual named Adawi Aimur-Noor Kuzbari. Translated, it means 'The Son of the Lion.' Mr. Kuzbari was born in Egypt and trained in Syria. We believe that Mr. Kuzbari was working with a pair of saboteurs that Homeland Security has named Abbott and Costello. We know next to nothing about them. They are ghosts. We suspect Abbott and Costello in several attacks on the infrastructure in the U.S. Abbott is the brains of the pair. He plans the attacks and does the training. Costello is the recruiter and enforcer. We suspect that Abbott and Costello are in the employ of a loosely-bound Middle Eastern organization called The Family. The Family is somewhat like a mafia. They work mainly in North Africa and the Middle East. They traffic in whatever high-value contraband will make them the most profit: drugs, gold, blood diamonds, young girls, slave labor, information, and, in the last couple of years, crude oil. While many are Islamic, they have no defined religious affiliation other than they recruit heavily from Islamic youth. They use violence to destroy their competitors and to cause focused terrorism to drive up prices and profits.

"Some operatives of The Family are also master recruiters. They play on whatever personal vendetta a potential enlistee might bear and they cite proof that their target competitor, usually the U.S., is to blame for their troubles. They are particularly good at pushing the emotional buttons of the weak-minded. The Family has three, and only three, operating goals: money, power, and influence. Again, we believe that Abbott and Costello are two of The Family's operatives.

"The FBI has been chasing these two ghosts for years. That is, until we obtained Mr. Kuzbari's body. We have to be covert when we search for information on the Kuzbari ID. The Family has sophisticated hackers and always seems to be a few steps ahead of us. We had the Canadian Border Services Agency run a driver's license border check on the Alex James ID. We wanted anyone watching to assume Mr. Kuzbari made it out of the Desert Canyons facility safely and then fled to Canada.

"French authorities recognized the Alex James counterfeit ID as the work of an Egyptian-born counterfeiter that they have been tracking for some time. The French gave us several names of other IDs that he has created and promised to keep us informed of any new IDs. This counterfeiter works exclusively for The Family. That's been our confirmation.

"One of the other IDs on the French hotlist surfaced in Las Vegas on the evening after the attack on Desert Canyons. He stayed in Las Vegas for two days and moved on before we could intercept him. A Las Vegas field team is trying to run down videos, pictures, or descriptions of him as we speak. So far, there's nothing tangible.

"Now, about Mr. Kuzbari's plan. Our computer forensics team has been working with Miss Spector since the incident. It seems that, early on, Ms. Spector identified a recurring anomaly in the daily reports from the access authority database. We coupled her information with an eyewitness account from Brian Sing, and have formulated what we suspect was Mr. Kuzbari's plan. He installed the remote trigger box in the primary coolant relief valve control circuitry. At this point in his plan, he died. We think that he next planned to open and disable a containment sump blow down valve in another room. The access reports then have him going to the River Water Pump House. We think that he was either going to establish a contaminated liquid waste discharge at one hundred percent concentration or get an accomplice to do it for him. The fact that he went to the pump house himself suggests that he intended to initiate a waste discharge himself. The fact that Dax and a student were in the pump house was a coincidence. We don't know what Mr. Kuzbari had planned for Dax and the student. As of right now, Dax is no longer under suspicion.

"With that done, the access report from the 22nd has Mr. Kuzbari returning to The Commons. We believe that his plan was to initiate the remote trigger by phone and then leave the plant from The Commons, with the other personnel, during the evacuation. Had Mr. Kuzbari succeeded, he would have released a great deal of contaminated sludge into the river, creating the worst single nuclear/ecological disaster in California history.

"We found Mr. Kuzbari's car in the back parking lot and moved it to one of the mechanical maintenance bays to give the illusion that Mr. Kuzbari has left the area. Now, the car wasn't interesting, per se. It was clean. It didn't even have any of Mr. Kuzbari's prints. He either wore gloves when he was in the car, or wiped it down every time he got out of it. However, we found a beer can on the passenger-side floor of the front seat. The lab report says that someone emptied and refilled the can with common tea. Mr. Kuzbari's prints were on the can. His thumb print was under the spout and his fingerprints were on the opposite side– the way one would hold the can when drinking from it.

"But there was also a second set of prints. A left thumbprint was on one side of the can, and the prints from the fingers of the left hand were on the other with the spout between them, faced away from the palm of the hand– the way one would hold the can while pouring tea into it. The prints of the fingers were unusable, but the thumbprint was perfect. We are certain that we have the thumbprint of whoever refilled that can with tea, and it wasn't Mr. Kuzbari. The thumbprint may be that of either Abbot or Costello. We have teams from police organizations around the world searching for a match.

"We found the apartment where Mr. Kuzbari lived. We watched it for 24 hours, and no one approached it. Inside, there was nothing. He did not even subscribe to a newspaper or magazine. The apartment was a dead end.

"Because of the thumbprint and the background information on the counterfeiter, we are closer to capturing Abbott and Costello than we have ever been.

"Our forensic computer team has been dissecting the computer code for the onsite door authorization software and they found a potential flaw in the verification format. The flaw was an acceptable compromise when management approved the onsite portion of the program. While the program itself has heavy security, it's what we call a lookup program. The onsite security program must access a personnel database maintained on a computer downtown to verify the access authority for each person swiping a card. The downtown personnel database has almost no security on it at all. Any one of a few dozen people could have accessed the database and changed either the authorizations or the personnel ID number for anyone in the database. Put it all together, and they could have made the changes without leaving an electronic trace.

"Mr. Kuzbari had help. We believe that someone downtown, with access to the personnel database, facilitated Mr. Kuzbari's unauthorized tour through the plant. We have a list of those who could have been the accomplice. We're conducting a low-key investigation of them all. We want to identify, capture, and question Mr. Kuzbari's accomplice."

Agent Corazal stopped for a few seconds to take a drink of water and let the crowd process the information that he had presented so far.

"Any questions before I go on?" he asked. While he waited for questions, he scanned the room. He tried to make eye contact with everyone in the room, to gauge their comfort level.

"Okay. Let's continue. An intelligence investigation is different from a criminal investigation. In a criminal investigation, our objective is to gather facts. In an intelligence investigation, we still want to gather facts, but we also want to know *things* without the opponent knowing we know them. We want to know the things that they know without them suspecting we do. We brought Mr. Kuzbari's car into the plant as soon as we could because we want them to think that Mr. Kuzbari survived the incident on May 1st and is currently trying to disappear. If they suspect that we have him, dead or alive, The Family may pull the plug on this team's U.S. operations, and they'll vanish.

"We also don't want them to know the extent of the damage to Desert Canyons or where we might place blame. We don't want them to guess a million other details. We want them to think that they were successful, that we're floundering in the fog, that we're incompetent, and that they have gotten away with it. We won't lie about the details, but we'll be selective about the truths that we present to the public."

Agent Corazal was about to continue, but stepped back, coughed once, and tried to clear his throat. After a couple of hard swallows, he said, "Excuse me. Where was I? Oh, yes. As an example, we will release that Mr. Downing suffered a mild Transient Ischemic Attack, a mild, harmless stroke. We will release that another employee developed some chest pains and trouble breathing. Mr. Downing was, in fact, transported by ambulance. We transported the heart-attack patient in a security vehicle from the remote parking lot. We're going to release that we transported both to the hospital in the same ambulance in case anyone saw two occupants in the ambulance. A quick check will verify that there were two people admitted to the hospital from Desert Canyons."

"As I said, this is a chess game. It succeeds if everyone is convincing with his or her version of the accepted script. The stories must be consistent."

Agent Corazal paused for a long moment and searched the faces before him. No one looked away. No one blinked. No one nodded. Agent Corazal didn't see any signs of disagreement. The FBI psychologists were satisfied with the reactions that they saw, as well. All the players seemed to be on board.

Agent Corazal continued, "I am going to read a worded press release. Take a copy before you leave. Please memorize the content. Please say nothing contrary or supplemental to the press release, especially to any public media. Don't say anything contrary to it on the phone with your sister. Don't show off at the local bar. Our success at catching Abbott and Costello may hinge on there not being one inconsistency in our stories."

Again, Agent Corazal paused.

He picked up a piece of paper and began to read, "At seven thirty in the morning on May 1st, Desert Canyons Nuclear Power Station had an unscheduled shut down of the main reactor. It occurred a few hours before the start of a scheduled refueling shutdown. A failure in one or more of the primary coolant safety systems, specifically the primary coolant relief valves, started a cascade of destructive events. A pilot-operated relief valve malfunctioned mechanically and became stuck in an intermediary position, which allowed a primary coolant relief valve to operate erratically. After an undetermined period of time, the relief valve opened, dumping enormous amounts of reactor cooling water into the containment sump. To compound the problem, a series of position indicating lights on the relief valves gave incorrect valve position information. The operating staff misinterpreted the erratic failure of the relief valve air pilot control valve and the misleading position light information. As a result, the operating staff misdiagnosed a 'Loss of Coolant Accident' and failed to take appropriate action. There was also a small, but unexplained, fire in one of the containment penetration rooms. The origin of the fire is under investigation. The combined result was some minor damage to the reactor itself.

"Desert Canyons Nuclear Power Station will be maintained in a 'Cold Shut Down' status, while we investigate these incidents and make repairs. All other containment safety systems operated as designed. Radioactive contamination did not escape the Containment Vessel. Radioactive contamination did not escape into the environment. No plant personnel reported injured or exposure to levels of radiation above normal operating standards. Further information on the schedule for the completion of the repairs will be provided as it becomes available. Two people were hospitalized during the event with non-life-threatening conditions. Both were treated and released."

Agent Corazal paused again, then said, "That's the press release. We don't want these people to know that we found the trigger box. It burned in the fire. Mr. Kuzbari triggered it as planned. We don't want them to think that we have Mr. Kuzbari. Mr. Kuzbari fled to Canada. We don't want them to think that we assume that the incident was anything but an unfortunate accident.

"Everyone is on board with this press release, yes?" Agent Corazal asked.

Agent Corazal's face softened. He continued, "I'm told that the air pilot valve that failed would have failed at some point in time, anyway. It was inevitable. However, it would have failed as an isolated event, not a part of a cascade of events. In that case, we would handle the incident within the purview of a normal operating procedure. Our analysis says that no damage would have occurred if the valve failure were an isolated event. The FBI medical examiner told me that the failure of this air valve might have been the triggering event for Mr. Kuzbari's heart failure. It seems that the timing of the failure of this little fifty-dollar air pilot valve may have been what thwarted the operation planned by Kuzbari. It may have been what saved Southern California from a nuclear disaster. It's a shame that, in our press release, we have to identify this air valve as the isolated point of failure that caused this meltdown." Agent Corazal couldn't say anything, but he was thinking *the timing of this valve failure was an act of divine intervention. I believe that God was on our side and was looking out for us at that instant.*"

As the main meeting broke up, Agent Corazal turned to Brian Sing. "Mr. Sing, in the past, you have displayed body language that telegraphs your disagreement with dissemination of misleading or incomplete information to the public. Has your opinion changed?"

Brian looked at Agent Corazal. "I can't believe that I'm saying this, but yes, it has. Considering everything that I know now, I'm convinced beyond any element of doubt that your course of action was for the greater good. I'm on board," he said.

Agent Corazal sat down and continued, "I'm not sure if you know, but Lenell, Christina, Dax and I were in Washington D.C. yesterday and met with the president, his cabinet, and some members of his Infrastructure Security Committee. The IFS subcommittee functions under the authority of the Homeland Security Act. Jack and Brian also briefed the president about the sabotage at Desert Canyons.

"The President has instructed NRC to fund the formation of a liaison office within this local utility. Brian will be the lead. The federal government will fund Brian's office, the utility will supply the business structure, and the FBI will provide the agenda. The first assignment for the liaison staff will be to attend infrastructure security meetings around the country and supply insight and expertise that will help the group achieve its security objectives. A majority of the focus for Homeland Security is identifying and neutralizing terrorist threats. The infrastructure security subcommittees will focus on specific areas of infrastructure vulnerability-food and water supplies, power, gas, highways, blood supply, etc. Each individual committee will work to identify vulnerabilities in their particular focus area and then make the infrastructure less vulnerable. The more inconvenient that we make it for terrorists to attack a particular area of the infrastructure; the more likely they are to move on to a softer target, maybe outside the U.S."

"We are making this a focus group, run by a private utility to lessen the appearance of federal involvement. We briefed Brian on the new assignment yesterday and authorized him to hire a support staff. Brian?"

Brian spoke, "The three of you are my first choice. We'll find others later. I can't tell you how impressed I was at the enormity of this endeavor. We have a huge job ahead of us. There'll be some travel and a lot of overtime. I don't foresee there being any public recognition. I do passionately believe that the security of our nation and our way of life is at stake. I know that you're the right people for this assignment, and would be honored if each of you would consider signing on."

Brian's choices were heartfelt. Too bad none of the three would ever work for Brian in the new assignment.

Dax didn't know it yet, but he would end up taking a lucrative operations assignment at a nuclear power plant on the banks of the Mississippi River in Louisiana, right across the river from the small town of La-Place. He would make the move because he felt he needed a more peaceful lifestyle.

Christina had already put a lot of consideration into quitting the utility, getting married, and starting a family. Today's incident had shaken Christina to the possibility that she might have been exposed to a damaging dose of radiation over the last few days. The past few days were a wake-up call for Christina. She was no longer willing to risk a radiation overdose. This assignment conflicted with her new life plan.

Lenell was also considering other options for her future and didn't think they included her being a high-paid, high-powered, national security consultant. She had already declined an offer from the FBI to join their Office of Computer Forensics as an analyst. That job meant relocation to D.C. She didn't see the wisdom to moving from a soft target into the heart of a high-profile, hard target.

Brian would start his new assignment alone. Of course, for Brian, this assignment beat being a low-level, part-time licensing advisor to the NRC.

Agent Corazal turned the conversation to a new topic, "Brian, this morning there was another new development concerning your new assignment. The president's chief of staff sent a message to both the directors of the FBI and the Department of Energy. In the message, he stated that the president was impressed with your briefing, knowledge, and conservative assessments. Your experience in the nuclear power industry is invaluable. He also liked that you served in the U.S. Army Nuclear weapons program. Once a soldier, always a soldier, right?

"By directive of the President of the United States, any action taken or instruction given by Brian Sing will have the full authority of the White House and the President of the

United States. Congratulations, Sir. You're now one of the president's most valued and influential advisors."

Agent Corazal stopped. Everyone was quiet. Lenell slowly searched the faces in the room. No one even blinked. Lenell looked at Brian. Everyone seemed to know that, even though the tip of a broadsword wasn't touched to Brian Sing's shoulders, the President of the United States just made him a Knight of the Realm.

"The president can count on me," Brian said.

Agent Corazal closed the meeting, and everyone stood up to leave. Each knew where he or she was going and what to do next, except Lenell. She had her new direction handed to her, but now she had a new dilemma. How was she going to get Brian Sing to notice her as more than a potential new staff member for his new office?

As they were all leaving the room, Brian turned to her and matter-of-factly asked, "Lenell, it's been a long day. Would you join me for dinner tonight?"

Just as easily, she answered, "Sure. How about we do home cooking at my place? I have a new recipe for jalapeño burritos. Say, seven o'clock?"

"Great. See you at seven," he answered and left.

In the hallway outside the conference room, the NRC inspector took Brian aside. "Mr. Sing," he said, "the President of the United States sends his greetings and asks if you would attend a summit on nuclear power infrastructure security in New York next Wednesday, Thursday, and Friday. The president's chief of staff asks that you brief the President by Sunday night. My office made the necessary travel arrangements and faxed you an itinerary. The commission's executive jet will be at your disposal until you return."

"Of course," Brian answered knowing that, at this time, he couldn't say no.

Christina, Dax, and Brian headed for the control room. There was still a lot of cleanup to coordinate. Jack, Agent Corazal, and the NRC inspector went to Jack's office to continue the debriefing. Lenell called her office assistant to tell her that she would be out of the office for the rest of the day. She had some shopping to do. She needed to buy the ingredients for jalapeño burritos. She also needed to find a recipe for jalapeño burritos.

*****

In LaPlace, Louisiana, Babar was sitting down to a computer to browse the dating bulletin boards. He was not in any big hurry. Within twenty minutes, Babar found what he was looking for. The ad read, "Belgian born, ballet-dancing bull rider seeks romantic contact with Knife Thrower. Call 16th at 12:00, New Orleans time 650-555-4756." Babar wrote the number down. He would decode the real number later, *can't have every nutcase on the east coast calling at 12:00*. He went through the rest of the bulletin boards with more urgency and with no success. He then turned on the news to see if there was anything new at Desert Canyons.

The FBI would never know just how perfectly their deception worked. On June 2nd, Babar read a new bulletin board posting from Gilbert. It was a request for an information update, not a request for contact. After the usual ridiculous opening, the message read, "House in the desert shut down permanently. Clown has disappeared. He may be in Canada. I'll find him. I will pay him what he is worth."

The Defect

Chapter Twenty-One

Seventy-five days after the accident at Desert Canyons, a co-worker of Bobby Joe Macon was in the Conyers County morgue to identify the body of Bobby Joe. Bobby Joe died of an accidental overdose of a combination of cocaine, alcohol, and an unidentified designer drug. For Bobby, minimum effort meant minimum life. He was thirty-six years old.

*****

At noon that same day, Babar Collins stood near the flagpole at the north end of the field at the Lake Pontchartrain Hot Air Balloon Festival. Gilbert Johnson walked toward him with a young woman in tow. "Babar, this is Bertie Bollings, a new friend. Bertie works at the SimCanCo Refinery in LaPlace. She wanted to meet you today. She wants to work with us."

Babar nodded and smiled his most gregarious smile as he shook her hand and said, "Bertie, can you give us a moment? I must speak with Gilbert." Bertie stepped a few paces away and turned to watch the spectacle of the balloon crews preparing their balloons.

"Gilbert, has any information on Alex James surfaced? Did you find him? Is he in custody? Is he dead?" Babar was more anxious than Gilbert had ever seen him. It showed in his face.

"No, Babar, we have found no mention or reference to Alex James. No word at all. His car has disappeared. There are clues that he may have fled to Canada. Every source of information I have says that the incident at Desert Canyons was an accident and a fire of unknown origin."

"Keep looking. For now, we can assume that he is in Canada, but we must act as though he is alive and in police custody. You are sure that he knew nothing that would lead the authorities back to us?" he asked.

When neither spoke, Babar asked, "Tell me of the girl."

"She works at the refinery. Management has passed her over for promotions and raises. She is angry and willing to help us for money. She says it is for money, but she seeks revenge. She will be a valuable asset. I assured her that she would never be caught and never be prosecuted," Gilbert reported.

Babar nodded, "Well done. Gilbert, find out which fire station would respond first to a fire at the party site. Find us an ally at that fire station."

Gilbert nodded and spoke, respect in his voice. "Agha, someone has been making inquiries into the background and financial status of Manuel Rojas. It is discrete and low level, but I must go to California today, and discuss Manuel's options with him in person. My plane leaves in two hours. I should be back tomorrow. Talk with Bertie; she has a great deal of information." Gilbert left without further word or gesture.

*****

"Bertie, it is a pleasure to meet you. Tell me of SimCanCo," Babar said.

"They will soon start building a fourth refining tower that will increase the production of the facility by thirty percent. They will be hiring a lot of temporary help. They have also been installing a new computer-based operating system that will allow any operator with the correct access codes to access any automatic controller in all four towers and change the operating instructions. Access to the control system can only be made from inside the refinery," she said. She leaned into him and looked far too serious.

"Smile! Don't be so serious. You look suspicious. Act like you are enjoying the day," he continued. He stepped a few steps away, gestured to the sky, and laughed aloud. A balloon shaped like a cartoon character was rising from the ground and beginning its leisurely ascent. He stepped closer to her, "Tell me everything," he instructed.

*****

Not more than fifty feet away, Special Agent Amada Mendoza Ruiz Diaz, FBI, stood at the base of the same hill eating an ice cream cone. As the newest Special Agent in the office, she was assigned most of the less glamorous assignments. At least it wasn't another Elvis sighting. She was young, runway-model-thin, and had a beauty that bespoke of her Cuban ancestry. Her smile was disarming and helped her blend into the crowd. She had been at the Balloon Festival for two hours, looking at the people around her. This wasn't like real work for Amanda. She loved looking at the people around her and wondering who they were.

A medium-credibility report had come into the field office that two or more Middle Eastern sympathizers were going to have a clandestine meeting at the festival today. There was no mention of what the meeting might be about, but the informant was sure that the FBI would be interested. Amanda was assigned to watch for them, identify them, photograph them, follow them to their cars, and record their license plates. Her assessment of the assignment was, *not likely*. No one at this festival seemed out of place. If they were here and if they were meeting, they were invisible.

Enough wasted time. She dropped the rest of her ice cream cone in the trash and started walking to her car. When she pulled up to the exit gate, there was one car in front of her: an older, blue Chevy driven by Gilbert Johnson. Gilbert waited for an opening in the traffic and then turned right to go to the New Orleans airport. Amanda watched the blue Chevy pull away, watched a few more cars go by, and then turned left to go home. She would file a surveillance report on Monday.

*****

Two hours later, Babar sat on a picnic bench digesting what he had heard from Bertie and watched the last of the festivities for the day. Bertie Bollings, disgruntled employee, wannabe terrorist, loser, had left. The balloons were all up and away. Most of the people had drifted off. The last of the balloon support crews loaded their hardware into their *chase* trucks. Babar stood up to leave. He was becoming conspicuous. He walked to his car like a man without a care in the world, more than satisfied with the information that he had gathered this day. A tentative plan was taking form. He was almost happy.

He got into his unlocked car, put the key in the ignition, and started it. The first whiff of air from the air conditioner assaulted him. It was horrible, like sour milk mixed with burning chocolate. He looked at his vent as though it might have a snake coming out of it. Then he realized that his doors were locked and the engine had stopped. His anti-theft system activated. He was trapped. It would take a call to the security company to open the door. The car alarm announced the situation to the people in the area. He exhaled as he realized that his eyes were beginning to burn, but he couldn't inhale. He coughed out once, but again, no breath seemed to come back in. He felt his chest expanding and thought he could feel the air going into his lungs, but there was no sensation of relief from the suffocation. He panicked and reached for the door handle. The handle moved fully, but wouldn't open. It was useless. People who heard the car alarm were grouping around the car. One man tried the door handle. Another tried to break the driver's side window. Babar screamed out the last bit of air. None would come back in. He knew that he had been poisoned and that he was dying. He alternated from pounding on the driver's side window to yanking at his seat belt, which the anti-theft circuit had also locked. He searched the crowd outside for help and found none. He tried to move into a standing position, as though it would free him of the seat belt. He tried to scream, but could not manage more than coughing some spittle on the inside of the windshield. As Babar's brain became more oxygen-deprived, he settled into his seat and seemed to go to sleep.

Finally, someone broke a window and reached in to pull him out of the car, but the damage was done. Babar's lungs were burned by the chemicals and had begun to secrete a sticky bodily fluid to soothe the burned area. The secretion also prevented oxygen from crossing the membrane into his blood stream. A dozen people watched Babar Collins suffocate.

*****

After the window was broken, a few people noticed the smell of sour milk, but no one had any negative side effects. The remnants of the poison dissipated into the evening air. The gas that had assimilated into Babar's body metabolized in a few minutes to the point of being undetectable during the autopsy. The autopsy results listed the cause of death as *respiratory failure of unknown cause.* His ID checked out, and no next of kin was ever found. Babar Collins was interred in Louisiana at the parish's expense two weeks later. The sheriff never examined the car.

If the thumbprint of a suffocation victim in Louisiana had ever been compared to a thumbprint on a beer can in California, the FBI would have had a field day.

Chapter Twenty-Two

The body of Manuel Rojas was found at nine the next morning in his backyard orchard. He had been pruning the fruit trees on a ladder. It appeared that that he had fallen ten feet to the ground when the limb that he was cutting had hit his ladder, knocking him to the ground. He fell on the back of his shoulders with his feet in the air. The problem was that he had fallen on a large, hard-tined orchard rake that penetrated his spine. It took several painful minutes for death to take him. The part that Manuel Rojas played in the Desert Canyons nuclear incident was never discovered publicly. Manuel never enjoyed one penny of his bank account in the Cayman Islands. The offshore bank account was liquidated and closed the next day.

*****

An hour and a half later, Gilbert Johnson boarded a plane at LAX, bound for New Orleans. He posted a bulletin board update saying that "The contract in California is signed. Everyone is in a happy place." Gilbert loved codes.

After he entered his post, he began to read the other daily postings and found one meant for him. The important part of the message read, "The king is dead, long live the king."

So his longtime friend, Babar Collins, was dead. He neither showed nor felt any emotion. This was as it should be. Gilbert knew a month ago that Babar was expendable. The day that The Family sent him a picture of Babar's left thumbprint on an Interpol wanted poster, Gilbert knew. While it was true that there were no fingerprints on file for comparison, Babar was sloppy to let the authorities obtain his fingerprint. He needed to be retired.

Gilbert's new handler/co-conspirator was responsible for this posting. This new member of this cell had met him four weeks ago and was assigned three tasks: First, she had to interact with Babar without him realizing that she was anything but a disgruntled American. Second, she had to kill Babar before she could take his place. Lastly, she (along with Gilbert) had to complete the LaPlace assignment.

*****

Gilbert Johnson knew that he had to change his way of doing business. Bertie Bollings, a.k.a. Faresta Sajadi, most recently from Canada, originally from Afghanistan, was as much a psychopath as Gilbert. He would have to watch his back with a great deal more diligence, and he would have to prove himself all over again. Gilbert didn't trust Bertie. He was concerned about the need for him to work with a mere woman. His life had changed, and he didn't relax for a second during his flight to Louisiana.

*****

Later that same beautiful afternoon, Brian Sing was standing and answering questions, yet again. He felt weak in the knees. His hands were shaking, and his mouth was dry. As he turned to face the assembly behind him, he had the most significant conscious moment of transition in his life to-date. Lenell took his hand, and a voice from behind him said, "Ladies and gentlemen, it is my pleasure to introduce Mr. and Mrs. Brian Sing."

*****

As Gilbert flew to New Orleans, and the body of Manuel Rojas was being loaded in the ambulance, Deputy Undersheriff for Dallas County, Texas, Tim Hayden, sat down at his desk to eat lunch and open some of the day's mail. First up was a pretty, lime green envelope with gold borders. *Expensive*, he thought. The letter was addressed to him and post-marked Los Angeles, California. There was no return address. Inside was a simple lime green card embossed on the front, in gold, with the words, "Thank You." Inside was a simple message written in ink, "Thank You." The undersheriff dismissed the card and its message with a snort of arrogance and dropped it into the shredder.

Epilogue

One year after the incident at Desert Canyons, a tow truck pulled up to a boat and trailer that had been abandoned behind a local apartment building. At the apartment building owner's request, the unlicensed boat and trailer were towed to a local wrecking yard for salvage.

*****

The forty-five caliber, semi-automatic handgun, in its vacuum-packed plastic bag, hidden among the rocks on the side of an access road at the now decommissioned Desert Canyons Nuclear Power Station was never found.

I hope you enjoyed my story. We struggling authors live by online reviews. I would very much appreciate if you could take some time and post a review on a couple of the more influential book sites:

Amazon.com
GoodReads.com
BarnesAndNoble.com

If you are unfamiliar with the process of posting reviews, email:

jeff.bailey4007@gmail.com

I'll talk you through it. I always enjoy hearing from a fan.

Also, if you decided to not keep this book in your personal library, please, don't discard it. Pass it on to someone else that might enjoy the read. Help keep this book alive. Everyone knows that by keeping a book alive and in circulation, you breed amazing good luck, save the environment, and promote world peace.

Thanks for your time!

Jeff

Following is an excerpt from the next book in this series. Hope you enjoy!

Not On MY Watch

Chapter One

The burning metal airframe super-structure hissed at Cassie. The cockpit of a fighter jet was tight to begin with, but once it was crumple in a crash, it was almost too snug to allow her to take a deep breath. The heat was unbearable. She inched forward, feeling her way through the swirling smoke, and tried to use her diaphragm and stomach to draw her breath instead of expanding her lungs. The roar of the flames overstimulated her hearing until all sound faded to white noise. She blew out a breath and pulled herself further into the burning structure. She tried to orient herself each time the occasional flashes of light from the flames penetrated the smoke enough for her to see shadows.

Cassie, Lance Corporal Cassandra Sing, USMC, estimated that one more squeeze into the void would bring her close enough to the pilot to feel for his body. An explosion sounded nearby, shaking the structure. The metal casement seemed to close in even tighter, intensifying her claustrophobia. The explosion also added to her sense of urgency. As if aviation fire rescue wasn't dangerous enough, Cassie was a US Marine aviation fire rescue specialist. When she fought an airplane fire or rescued a pilot, there was the possibility of live bullets and bombs in the plane. The explosion meant that she had to hurry. Burning flight fuel, bullets, and bombs don't play well together.

Cassie maneuvered onto her side and reached forward with her free hand, making it even harder to draw a breath. But her effort was rewarded. She felt the slack face of the Marine pilot just out of sight in the darkness. She pulled the small rescue-breathing mask from the Velcro connector on the shoulder of her canvas fire jacket and fitted it over the pilot's face. Procedures dictated that she first protect the pilot's ability to breathe whenever there was a possible nuclear weapon or nuclear material onboard the aircraft. Aspirated radioactive metals wreak havoc on the human body. With the mask in place, she reached back down to her waist, retrieved her field knife, and cut the pilot free of his harness. The heat was beginning to leach through her fire jacket.

The pilot fell against Cassie like a sack of wet sand and pinned her head against the metal structure. The loss of that tiny bit of space compounded her growing claustrophobia. Another small shot of panic coursed through her as the adrenaline hit her blood stream. She couldn't suppress a little scream. The roar of the fire consumed the sound. She could not give in to panic. A fellow Marine's life was at stake. She would not falter.

After blowing out another breath, she inched her way back out the way she entered, pulling the deadweight of the pilot behind her. *Breathe, scoot, pull, breathe, scoot, pull.* She had a long way to go.

As she moved, she heard the report of a mind-jarring klaxon horn from somewhere outside the burning fuselage.